WITHDRAWN

P9-AGU-751

Phantom Outlaw
AT Wolf Creek

Children's Books by
Sigmund Brouwer

FROM BETHANY HOUSE PUBLISHERS

THE ACCIDENTAL DETECTIVES

The Volcano of Doom
The Disappearing Jewel of Madagascar
Legend of the Gilded Saber
Tyrant of the Badlands
Shroud of the Lion
Creature of the Mists
The Mystery Tribe of Camp Blackeagle
Madness at Moonshiner's Bay
Race for the Park Street Treasure
Terror on Kamikaze Run
Lost Beneath Manhattan
The Missing Map of Pirate's Haven
The Downtown Desperadoes
Sunrise at the Mayan Temple
Phantom Outlaw at Wolf Creek
Short Cuts

WATCH OUT FOR JOEL!

Bad Bug Blues
Long Shot
Camp Craziness
Fly Trap
Mystery Pennies
Strunk Soup

www.coolreading.com

Accidental DETECTIVES

Phantom Outlaw
at Wolf Creek

SIGMUND BROUWER

BETHANYHOUSE
MINNEAPOLIS, MINNESOTA

Phantom Outlaw at Wolf Creek
Copyright © 2005
Sigmund Brouwer

Cover illustration by Chris Ellison
Cover design by Lookout Design Group, Inc.

All rights reserved. No part of this publication may be reproduced, stored in a retrieval system, or transmitted in any form or by any means—electronic, mechanical, photocopying, recording, or otherwise—without the prior written permission of the publisher and copyright owners.

Published by Bethany House Publishers
11400 Hampshire Avenue South
Bloomington, Minnesota 55438

Bethany House Publishers is a division of
Baker Publishing Group, Grand Rapids, Michigan.

Printed in the United States of America

Library of Congress Cataloging-in-Publication Data

Brouwer, Sigmund, 1959-
    Phantom outlaw at Wolf Creek / by Sigmund Brouwer.
        p.   cm. — (Accidental detectives)
    Summary: While visiting a ranch in Montana, Ricky finds God's presence comforting when his investigation of disappearing livestock puts his life in danger.
    ISBN 0-7642-2578-2 (pbk.)
    [1. Ranch life—Fiction. 2. Christian life—Fiction. 3. Mystery and detective stories.]
I. Title II. Series: Brouwer, Sigmund, 1959- . Accidental detectives.
    PZ7.B79984Ph   2005
    [Fic]—dc22   2004020611

SIGMUND BROUWER is the award-winning author of scores of books. He speaks to kids around the continent in an effort to instill good reading and writing habits in the next generation. Sigmund and his wife, Cindy Morgan, divide their time between Tennessee and Alberta, Canada.

For Olivia
and the sunshine you bring
into this world

There can only be one reason for riding a Greyhound bus through the middle of nowhere trying to keep tabs on someone as terrifying as Joel, my six-year-old brother.

Stupidity.

"Ricky Kidd," my mother had begun in a grave tone two days earlier as we sat at the kitchen table.

Hearing it then, I knew I was in trouble. She had spoken with the tone grown-ups use whenever they want to convince you to do something you ordinarily regard as crazy. Because if it's good for you, they don't beat around the bush.

"You're twelve years old now," she continued, then put her hands across the table on top of mine to look at me earnestly.

Major league trouble looms when they do that.

"And Rachel is a baby," I replied to Mom. My little sister was very, very sweet. Unlike, say, the brother in the middle. "Joel is six. Now that we've confirmed all our ages, it's probably time for me to go and count the clippings in my toenail collection."

She continued as if I hadn't said a word, which confirmed that she had the conversation all planned out. "And it's time you made responsible decisions all by yourself."

"Great," I said. I knew I wouldn't be able to squirm out of this, but a person shouldn't give up easily. "Does that mean I can borrow the car tonight?"

"I'm being serious," she warned, taking her hands back.

"So was I. I won't drive faster than forty miles an hour unless—"

"It's about your brother. With Mike and Ralphy already at the ranch, he'll only have Rachel, and as you pointed out, she's just a baby. For all practical purposes, Joel will be all alone here as soon as you leave."

Exactly.

The fact that Joel wouldn't be there was half the reason I was so excited about the upcoming trip.

As a brother, I'll admit Joel's okay. He even wears white high-top sneakers, blue jeans, and T-shirts because he wants to copy me. But Joel's worse than a tiny ghost. Ralphy and Mike, who were waiting for me on Mike's uncle's ranch, are twelve, too, and we still know better than to relax when Joel's around.

It's like this. Give Joel a choice between eating hot dogs or spying on us, and the dilemma would put him into agony. So he'll find a way to do both. Locked doors and closed windows never seem to stop him. Worse, you need radar to know when he's following you.

Joel never says much when you do manage to spot him. He just stares and watches. He disappears as soon as you turn your head and then appears again when you least expect it. Which is usually when you're doing something you shouldn't.

"Poor little guy," my mom had continued two days earlier in the kitchen, pouring me more milk and pushing chocolate chip cookies across the table. *As if I can't recognize bribery.* "He admires you so much. A month alone here will seem like a lifetime to him."

How could I explain that a month with him usually seems like a lifetime to me?

"I really think you should ask him to come along," she said sweetly. "You and your friends will be having so much fun, it wouldn't be any trouble to include him."

I opened my mouth to utter the only objection that might work, but she was quicker.

"And Mike's aunt and uncle don't see it as a problem. In fact, they said they'd love to have extra company."

Shot down before leaving the ground. Why did I have the feeling this was a well-planned campaign?

"But, of course, Ricky," she said with a smile, "this decision is entirely up to you. You're mature enough to know what's right."

I hesitated.

"Aren't you." She made it sound like a statement.

I was ready to wear diapers to prove maturity had nothing to do with the issue. Unfortunately, at that moment I happened to glance out the kitchen window.

Joel was sitting against the big oak tree in our backyard. His teddy bear, a battered brown with gray-white paws and a white button for the left eye and a black button for the right eye, was beside him. The teddy bear had a handkerchief tied around its neck, as if it were a miniature cowboy.

That teddy bear is Joel's only weakness. When I'm mad at Joel, I remind him that teddy bear stuffing is hard to replace. It gets his attention. But I could never hurt the bear because I remember Joel's face the day Old Man Jacobsen's dog snuck away with it. Joel began digging with his plastic toy garden shovel in all the dog's favorite hiding spots. He wouldn't let me help. Even the dog was smart enough to stay out of sight. Joel's face was muddy with tears and dirt by the time he found the teddy bear. Then he gave it to me to wash, and we were both happy.

Thinking of that day made me sentimental. A mistake.

Seeing Joel against the tree made me more sentimental. A bigger mistake.

Joel had his knees tucked against his chest, with his arms around his knees. He gently rocked back and forth, staring into the distance.

A quick lump hit my throat. The poor guy *would* be alone for a month. Endless hours with nothing to do except wonder about the fun he was missing. How could I think of being mean?

"Sure, Mom," I had said across the kitchen table. "I'll take him."

I looked outside at the tree again. Joel had disappeared.

Now I was on the bus, and it rumbled below me as it rolled, its vibrations gently rocking me between daydreams and sleep.

West on Interstate 90 was our direction. We'd already been traveling most of the day, cutting through South Dakota and now Wyoming. Lots of land, hardly any people.

Hours and hours ahead, in Montana, was a city called Butte, which rhymes with "cute." There we would transfer to another Greyhound bus going south on Interstate 15. Mike's uncle's ranch was in the mountain valleys north of the Idaho border. Our arrival time would be sometime late at night.

I had already finished one book. Instead of reading more, I had propped my folded jacket against the window and used it as a pillow. Whenever I woke and opened my eyes, I could stare at the land that stretched forever to a faraway horizon. Something about it gave me a good kind of restlessness, as if being out there under all that blue sky would fill my lungs with freedom.

Horses, I thought. *Cowboys and horses and wide open—*

I had another thought. This one terrible. Where was that reassuring pressure against my leg, the heavy warmth that meant Joel was right beside me, napping with his teddy bear?

Nuts. No warmth. No Joel.

I stood so quickly I banged my head against the luggage rack.

"Joeeel," I whispered as my eyes watered. "Where arrrrre yooouuuu?"

Nothing.

I stayed calm. He *had* to be on the bus. Where else could he be, right? Unless—the thought chilled me instantly—I had slept through one of the scheduled stops.

No way, I told myself. He wouldn't wander away and watch the bus depart without him. But then again, it was Joel.

I tripped across a fat lady's leg. She scowled. I smiled an apology and backed away, only to elbow an old man on the other side of the aisle.

I smiled nervously at him and slowly worked my way up the aisle, swaying to the roll of the bus. Who would think a Greyhound could be so long?

Two bikers with long, greasy hair, muscle shirts, and tattoos. A half dozen white-haired old ladies. Three mothers with babies. The old man I had elbowed, the fat lady who was using two seats, a bunch more grown-ups sleeping with their faces buried, one sleeping with his head back and a fine line of drool down his chin, and the bus driver. But no Joel.

Wonderful.

I got on my knees to look under the seats and crawled down the aisle on the way back to my seat. People stared at me, but finding Joel was more important than me looking normal. All I saw were shoes, boots, and a few legs with varicose veins. No Joel.

We had been sitting close to the back of the bus. There were only two rows behind my seat. Both were empty.

That left the washroom. I tried the door. Locked.

"Joel, are you okay?" Nothing.

I banged lightly. "Are you in there?"

I banged harder. "Joel! Answer me!" I rained a steady barrage against the door. Finally the doorknob turned. With a surge of relief, I grabbed it and yanked the door. And stopped with my mouth open.

"Don't they teach city slickers no manners? Even puppy dogs learn to wait their turn."

I stared face level at a guy my age. Boots, tight faded jeans, blue jean jacket with collar up to his face, and a pushed-low cowboy hat.

"I, uh, thought it was someone else," I stammered.

"Really? So you can see through doors? That's a neat trick."

"No, I meant . . ." I stopped. "Look, why didn't you say something when I was banging on the door?"

"'Cause whoever was making that racket could wait."

My face burned hot red. "I'm sorry. Really. Very sorry."

He shook his head in disgust and walked past me to sit right behind my seat. He slouched back, dropped his cowboy hat on his face, and ignored the bus and the world.

Which left me not only feeling stupid, but without Joel.

CHAPTER 2

There was only one thing to do.

I approached the bus driver. There was gray sprinkled in his short brush cut, and his belly banged the steering wheel every time the bus hit a bump. I stood there, waiting for him to notice me.

"Yes, kid," he finally said with resignation.

"My brother's lost, sir."

"I hope you find him."

"No, I mean he was on the bus, and now he isn't. That kind of lost."

"We don't baby-sit."

Which wasn't true. There were forms and stuff for two kids traveling. The driver *was* supposed to watch out for us.

"I'm scared maybe he got off at the last stop and didn't get back on," I said.

"So it was *your* lousy baby-sitting." The driver was starting to sound nervous. We both knew this wasn't good.

"I think I was asleep," I answered.

He sighed. "So what are you asking me to do?"

"Make a call. Maybe he's—"

"We're out of cell phone range."

Suddenly I was desperate. The bus driver didn't know how easily Joel could get in trouble. Every minute away from our last stop was another minute for Joel to disappear farther.

"Please stop the bus," I said.

"What?" He half turned in the seat.

"I need to get off the bus. I'm sorry, but I've got to find a phone right away. Maybe at a farmhouse or something." I tried the only weapon I had. "And I'm sure the newspapers will find it interesting about how much help you gave me in looking for a lost six-year-old kid."

"I hate this job," the bus driver muttered. He took a deep breath to calm himself. "Kid, do you see any farmhouses?"

I shook my head. Land, empty land, stretched as far as I could see. We really were in the middle of nowhere.

"So if I drop you off, where are you going to find a phone?"

"I don't know," I said stubbornly. "I'll walk. The newspapers will understand, I'm sure."

We were approaching an intersection. The driver wasn't too polite about slowing down. He slammed the brakes to cut hard to make the corner. I grabbed a rail to keep my balance. Behind me, passengers grumbled.

The driver reached for a microphone. "Unscheduled stop, folks. We have to find a farmhouse to make an emergency phone call."

The rumbling of wheels against asphalt was now a clacking of flying stones as we sped down a gravel road. I didn't dare turn around to face any of the other passengers.

"I hope you're satisfied, kid," the bus driver said. He glanced in the rearview mirror. "It doesn't look like many people back there are happy about this unscheduled detour."

I didn't say anything. I was too busy praying. Not that I think a person should be asking God for miracle solutions. You can't expect to be handed a parachute out of midair just because you're falling and praying at the same time, even though God could do it if He wanted to, I'm sure, but ... Instead, I was praying for Joel's safety. And for mine, which looked necessary with such a grumpy bus driver.

"Kid, your brother can't be that important if you're sleeping on your feet," he said.

I opened my eyes. "Good one, sir."

We were already far from the highway and moving down a hill. The road ahead was a lonely ribbon fading into the distance.

Where is a telephone? Doesn't anybody live around here?

"This better be a good emergency," someone said from behind us. "My ticket doesn't say anything about a scenic tour."

"If you call this scenic, you been living on the moon," somebody else shouted.

My ears burned. I tried not to think about the consequences of Joel wandering alone at some rough truck stop.

Finally we spotted a low-slung farmhouse against the sky. The driver slowed his bus and painfully cranked on the steering wheel to make the tight turn onto the dirt road that wound down to the house.

The big Greyhound jounced and rocked all of us as it pounded against the hard ruts of the packed dirt.

"Easy on my bones, man!" It was one of the tattooed guys.

"I'm going to kill you, kid." The bus driver gritted his teeth. "And then I'm going to kill your brother."

If we find him in time, I thought.

The dirt road ended at the front door of the farmhouse. The wood was gray-white from years in the sun without any paint. Its roof sagged and the steps on the front porch were falling apart.

The air brakes of the huge bus let out a whoosh as we stopped. The bus settled on its springs.

"I hope you're happy, kid," the driver snarled. "In case you didn't notice, this here driveway just ends. A person couldn't turn a Volkswagen around, let alone a twelve-ton bus."

I shrank. He was right. But we needed to save Joel.

"Which means I gotta go in reverse the whole way out," he continued. "That's nearly half a mile. When we get stuck, you're gonna push. Got that, kid? *If* I even let you stay on the bus."

He swung open the door and scowled at me. "Stay here, kid. I'll make the telephone—"

The screen door of the farmhouse slammed open. An old lady in a long checked dress trotted down the broken boards of the front porch, holding her dress high to keep from tripping. She met the driver just as he stepped out of the bus.

"Praise the Lord, you're here," she said between gasps.

"My feelings, too, lady. You got a telephone?"

"That's why we needed you," she said, a puzzled look rearranging the wrinkles on her face.

The bus driver shot a murderous glance at me. "I don't have time for chitchat, lady. I gotta make a phone call and then get this bus back on schedule."

She said, "I told you. Our telephone doesn't work. Which is why

I been praying five hours solid for you."

"Me?"

She nodded frantically. "You or anyone who could drive us out of here."

"Us?"

The old lady tugged on his arm. "Us," she said firmly. "And we don't have much time to waste." She pulled the bus driver to the house. He moaned.

That left me standing alone at the front of the bus and about forty people muttering in their seats behind me. I definitely did not dare turn around.

No telephone?

I sat in the driver's seat and slumped forward from the exhaustion of worrying. The horn blared, and I nearly had a heart attack.

"Ain't you done enough damage, kid?" someone called.

Before I could answer, the driver and the old lady came hurrying from the farmhouse again. Between them they led a young woman. It looked like she had three pillows stuffed under her dress.

"Clear the way!" the driver shouted. His face was flushed with excitement. "Make room for a miracle!"

The passengers in the front seats of the bus made room for the three of them as they entered.

As he expertly inched the bus backward down the long dirt drive-way, the bus driver explained. His face looked different now, like he was a knight charging ahead on a white horse. Which maybe he was.

"The old lady's seen a lot of babies being born," he said. "She says this one's going to be the worst. If they don't get to a doctor, the girl might die."

He stared intently at one side mirror and then the other, and gunned the motor to get more speed in the reverse gear. There was excited murmuring behind us in the bus as people tried making the young woman comfortable.

"Storm yesterday knocked out the telephone," the bus driver continued tersely. "Husband's a truck driver, hauling a load of plastic somewhere in Georgia. Their car won't start. And there was no way either could start walking for help. They figured on having maybe two, three hours left."

We were almost to the gravel road that led back to the highway.

The bus driver grinned at me. "So they prayed and prayed for a miracle, kid. Which was us."

He backed onto the gravel road, then swung the nose of the bus ahead and revved the motor.

"I've never been much of a believer, kid, but this changes things as far as I'm concerned."

A bus loaded with passengers showing up from the middle of nowhere was definitely a miracle as far as I was concerned, too. But I couldn't grin back, even as the bus was speeding along the gravel, bringing the woman and her baby to safety.

Joel was missing. I needed a telephone as soon as possible. Would the one at the hospital be soon enough? *Please, Lord, be with him, just as you are with the girl and her baby.*

"We're going to be moving pretty fast, kid. Maybe you should get back to your seat."

"Yeah," I mumbled. I couldn't blame the driver for overlooking my lost kid brother as he concentrated on his mission.

The cowboy my age pushed his hat up slightly to look at me as I reached my seat.

"So you're the goof who sent us packing around the countryside," he said.

Something about him looked funny, but I couldn't quite place what it was. Not the way he sat, not his face, not even the way he shot his chin forward stubbornly. But something.

I didn't have time to decide. "Yes, I'm the goof," I said. "But if your brother was missing, you'd do stupid things, too, so knock it off."

"If my brother was missing, instead of being such a goof, I'd look harder."

"Wha—"

"Short brown hair, teddy bear?" he said.

"How did—"

He pointed at the luggage rack above us, just ahead in the aisle. A tiny hand held the teddy bear. Beside it, Joel's head stuck out from between two suitcases as he studied the action and excitement at the front of the bus.

CHAPTER 3

"Atknuckle's ranch! Atknuckle's ranch!"

Nuts. Look away for one second, and he takes off again.

It was Joel, headed up the aisle. Correction, it was "Joel the Hero" headed up the aisle.

Instead of absolutely killing me, the bus driver had messed my hair affectionately when I finally broke the news to him in front of the hospital about finding Joel in the luggage racks.

"I'll buy the kid a medal. The girl's going to be just fine," he had laughed. "Now get back on the bus. We got some time to make up."

It might have been days before anyone stopped by that desolate farmhouse. There was no doubt God had worked a miracle to save the woman and her baby. Except, as I watched Joel toddle up the aisle, I think God saw more humor in the way He had managed the miracle.

Because Joel the Hero was making a lot of noise.

Normally, he makes mice seem as loud as marching bands. Joel doesn't talk much, and when he does, he says as little as possible. Not because he's slow. He already knows how to read, and even print out complete sentences, and he knows more words than most kids his age. But he's shy, and he mispronounces words once in a while, so he gets his out-loud sentences over with as fast as he can.

Except now he had all those new friends on the bus to introduce to his teddy bear.

Wonderful.

"Atknuckle's ranch," he said proudly, stopping at every row to shake his teddy bear at each new person. "Atknuckle's ranch for us."

The good part was that when Joel returned, he had pockets full of chocolate bars and gum. I guess being a hero was worth more than I thought.

"Hey, kid, where did you say you were headed?"

It was the cowboy my age in the seat behind me. "I didn't say," I said without turning around. "Besides, you seem like you know everything, so why don't *you* tell *me* where we're headed."

I couldn't explain why I felt a rivalry with the cowboy. I don't think it was being the same age. It was something else. And it was a weird kind of rivalry, with a tension underneath that I didn't understand.

He moved out of his seat. Exasperation, faded blue denim, and cowboy hat filled the aisle beside me as he stared down at Joel and me.

"I wasn't talking to you," he said. "I was talking to the kid with the teddy bear. The smart one."

I gritted my teeth. Once again, I was stuck with nothing to say.

The cowboy grinned at my brother. "So where you headed, kid?"

Joel, the little traitor, took a shine to the cowboy right away. "Atknuckle's ranch."

Aunt and uncle's ranch. But I wasn't going to explain that to the kid with the cowboy hat and the attitude.

We were going to be visiting George and Edith Andrews. They had invited their nephew and my best friend, Mike Andrews, plus Ralphy Zee and me for a summer visit. For all I cared, Joel could call their ranch "spaghetti." I just knew getting there instantly wasn't going to be soon enough. And, two hours short of Butte, Montana, and one hour behind schedule, we still had miles to go.

"Great, kid," the cowboy said to Joel. "I'm going to a ranch, too. Put it there." The cowboy stuck out his hand. Which I ignored. Joel reached over and gravely shook hands. *And* gave him a chocolate bar. The rat.

"Well, kid, I transfer in Butte, so I'm going to grab a little sleep before then. Enjoy your summer." The cowboy grinned crookedly at Joel. "And take care of your older brother."

The bright moon threw crisp shadows behind each wood tele-phone pole as we cruised down the interstate. I stared out the bus window, mesmerized by the blackness of the sky and the whiteness of the piercing stars.

The highway ran south from Butte through wide valleys. I almost shivered at the beauty of the mountains and the foothills on both sides, outlined dark and sharp by the strength of the moon. I could hardly wait for daylight to see the hills against blue sky.

Joel was finally asleep, teddy bear tucked under his arm.

WOLF CREEK 35 MILES, the last sign had read. I couldn't sleep. We were so close to being there.

On the opposite side of the aisle, the cowboy whom Joel liked was also staring out his window. He had only grunted at me with surprise to see us on the same bus leaving Butte, then ignored me to chat with Joel.

Which didn't bother me. Why would I want to be friends with someone like him?

Unfortunately, neither of us expected the welcoming committee that was waiting ahead.

It was one o'clock in the morning when we arrived at the truck stop in Wolf Creek. The bus rumbled as it geared down, but that didn't wake Joel. He stirred only after I pulled the teddy bear from his arm, and then he stared mournfully at me with accusing eyes.

"Atknuckle's ranch?"

"Sure, Joel. Whatever you say. We're here."

I stood to grab my luggage and nearly bumped the cowboy as he reached for his.

"Hmmppphh," he said. "If this is where you're getting off, remind me to keep a couple of ranches' worth of distance between us."

"No problem," I said. "If you stay upwind, I'm sure I'll be able to smell you in time."

Heh, heh. Finally got in a good one on him.

He laughed. "Not bad." Then he elbowed me out of the way and marched off the bus.

"Come on, Joel."

"See Atknuckle," he said with a vigorous nod.

"Sure."

We stepped off the bus, and it left immediately.

What I saw told me there had to be a mistake. Mike and Ralphy were standing outside the bus on the gravel parking lot. So were Mike's aunt and uncle, George and Edith. I recognized them from photos Mike had shown me from previous visits.

The mistake was that the cowboy from the bus was hugging Mike's aunt Edith.

I dropped my luggage in disbelief.

"Where Atknuckle?" Joel said eagerly.

The cowboy gave Mike's uncle George a big hug. Didn't shake hands. *Gave a hug.*

"Atknuckle?" a little more quietly from beside me.

The cowboy then hugged Mike. I thought real cowboys roped cows or shot at outlaws, instead of hugging everybody in sight.

Mike caught the look on my face. He smirked and walked over to me, leaving the cowboy by Ralphy and his aunt and uncle.

We've been friends for too long. I'd seen that smirk before. I said, "Not a friend of yours, by any chance?"

"Sort of," he said. "From Wyoming. I guess that was along your route."

Joel tugged at my sleeve. "Can't see Atknuckle," he stated.

"Atknuckle?" Mike asked.

"Let me get this straight," I said, ignoring his question and remembering how stupid I had looked to the cowboy during the bus ride. "You knew someone else was coming and forgot to tell me about him?"

Something about my question broadened the smirk on Mike's face. He giggled and walked away. He brought his uncle and aunt, Ralphy, and his cowboy cousin back with him.

"Ricky and Joel, I would like you to meet my aunt and uncle, Edith and George."

"How do you do?" I said politely.

"*They're* staying with us?" the cowboy broke in. "The kid said he was going to *Atknuckle's* ranch."

I was ready to faint from confusion.

"No Atknuckle?" Joel said, disappointed.

Ralphy said, "Atknuckle. Atknuckle." He snapped his fingers.

"Aunt and uncle," I said. "Aunt and uncle's ranch."

Joel comprehended. He smiled at everyone, happy to have found his Atknuckle.

The cowboy and I locked glances.

Mike said, keeping his face innocent, "And by the way, Ricky, I'd like you to meet my cousin—" he paused slightly—"Sarah."

He reached over, plucked the cowboy hat off his cousin's head, and set it at a jaunty angle over his own ears. The shadow from the brim of the hat could not hide his grin.

Lustrous red hair tumbled down to her shoulders.

CHAPTER 4

"It's Great Red," the old trapper whispered with fear in his voice as the monstrous grizzly bear backed us against the rock wall at the cliff's base. "He's been the terror of Wolf Creek valley for years."

I gulped.

"It's been good knowing you, kid," the trapper said.

The bear charged.

Suddenly it was completely dark and a terrible weight pressed upon me. I couldn't breathe. Fur filled my face.

I woke up clawing for daylight and scrambling in panic. The terrible weight on my face calmly slid down to my chest. Then yawned. Why a stupid fat farm cat would choose me as a warm place to sleep is beyond me.

We stared balefully at each other. I spit two cat hairs from my mouth.

Sunlight poured into the room between wide-open white curtains. The bed next to me was empty. Joel, of course, was gone.

The farm cat circled my chest, as if waiting for me to fall asleep again.

Wonderful. *Cat lovers of the world please forgive me*, I said silently, then yanked as hard as I could on the bedcovers. Fat or not, the cat scrambled for safety and jumped to the floor. It huffed at me and left the room slowly and with much dignity.

If only I could do that to Mike for not warning me about his cousin Sarah. I had a feeling she would be more trouble than Lisa Higgins, a friend back in Jamesville.

Dreaming of red grizzlies should have been no surprise to me. Mike's hair, like his cousin's, is red. Like a grizzly, he's a dangerous friend to have. He thinks the word *impossible* applies to anything that grown-ups don't want kids to try. Like juggling chain saws. Any grown-up will tell you it's impossible to juggle chain saws. Which, of course, it is.

If you told Mike it's impossible to juggle chain saws, he'd look through all the garages in our town of Jamesville to borrow enough to begin his act, then find a place to charge admission, and somehow make it look like my idea.

He's also got this rule about sneakers—they can't match. His left shoe is always a different color than his right shoe, and he has more pairs to choose from than I have comic books. At least it seems that way. I just wish sometimes the shoes would match the colors of his Hawaiian shirts. When he whizzes by on a skateboard, it hurts my eyes to watch him.

Usually, I forgive him for any trouble. He's a little bigger than I am.

I wasn't sure if I could forgive him this time, though. As if somebody could *forget* to mention his cousin would be on the same bus as I was. As if somebody could *forget* to mention his cousin was a girl.

"Hey, chowder head, wake up." A pillow came flying through the doorway. Mike grinned his crazy grin, the one that always gets him out of trouble.

"Breakfast," he said. "And believe me, they know how to make them out here."

Ralphy waved briefly as he followed Mike, hopping and pulling up his pants as he passed the doorway to my bedroom. He fell, thumping the floor hard.

Poor Ralphy. Computer whiz and science genius, but sometimes klutzy and always nervous. He's the one who will get stuck halfway up a tree or get his shirt caught on the Bradleys' fence just as their German shepherds come rushing up to bark at us.

He is skinny, with straight hair that points in every direction except for where it's supposed to. The back of his shirt always hangs out, and he gets yelled at for it by his older sisters, who spend so much time painting their fingernails and worrying about what dress to wear that I'm surprised they can find the time to yell at him. They yell at him a lot, and they sneak up behind him every time they have something to yell about, so we understand why he's the nervous type.

Ralphy muttered to himself as he rolled to his feet in the hallway. I stood and stretched, surveying my new home.

Like the rest of the ranch house, the bedroom was big. It had shiny dark hardwood floors. The furniture was a nice kind of old—classic, my mom would call it.

It was a two-story house with wide hallways, high ceilings, and a front porch that faced the west to catch sunsets. Mike and Ralphy slept in the other upstairs bedroom.

Sarah—I winced to think of the bus trip—and Mike's aunt and uncle had the downstairs bedrooms.

The most important room in the entire house was, of course, the kitchen. From it, the smell of sizzling bacon wafted through the air.

It didn't help that Sarah sat beside me at breakfast, elbowing me twice to make room as she sat down.

Everyone was around the breakfast table except Mike's uncle and Joel. Sarah's thick red hair made the morning sunlight dance. Unlike Mike, she did not have any freckles to match the hair. Her eyes were light green and bright, but her face seemed dark, as if she were mad at the world.

"Good morning," I said.

"Hmmph. Eagle Eye, the world's best baby-sitter," she said to me.

Not the world's most bubbly person in the morning, is she, I thought. *I can hardly wait until Joel pulls a stunt on her.*

Before I could think of a smart reply, Aunt Edith—at the bus depot, she had insisted we all call her Aunt Edith—set down in front of me a plate filled with scrambled eggs and pancakes.

She was tall, with peppered-gray hair pulled tight. Somehow she reminded me of the mountains behind the ranch. Her beauty came from the strength she radiated with her calm, competent manner. She wasn't photograph-beautiful. Not pretty, not dainty, not frilly. But beautiful from what the years had done to her face, leaving gentle lines of humor and caring. The person I would go to first if I ever got into trouble.

"Eat hearty," she told me with a grin. "Few things are as satisfying as seeing a young person enjoy food. What with our own boys all grown up, it's a sight I don't get the pleasure of near enough."

What is it about a grin that can say so much about a person? Her warmth filled the entire kitchen.

The porch door creaked open and then banged shut. Uncle George reached the entrance to the kitchen and filled the doorway as his voice filled the kitchen. "Morning, folks." He scratched his chest and yawned. "Another nice day out there."

Uncle George had a broad face under dark straight hair, and strong white teeth that made his grin seem even huger than it was. He pulled his suspenders from the front of his chest and let them go with a snap. "You kids leave any breakfast? I'm hungry enough to chase down a coyote and eat it raw."

He took a step into the kitchen.

"George," Aunt Edith said. "We've been married twenty-six years, and every morning I still have to point out that you forgot to remove your boots."

"Honey, I keep them on just to hear you say exactly that." He winked at the rest of us. "Your pretty voice sends shivers up and down my spine."

He left his boots on and walked over and gave her a big smooch on the forehead.

Sarah shook her head and went back to eating. *What is with that girl?*

Uncle George kicked off his boots, skidding them across the kitchen into the porch. "Now," he said, "let me dig in."

Uncle George pulled up to the table. "Great looking breakfast, Edith," he shouted across the kitchen. "Glad you didn't marry anyone else."

"I was too young to know better," she laughed back. "And now I'm too set in my ways."

There was a friendly silence for a few minutes as we waited for Uncle George to pray before his meal.

He spoke to me next.

"That brother of yours always so quiet?" Uncle George asked me between gulps of steaming coffee.

I nodded. *Where* had *Joel gone so early in the morning?*

"Thought so," he said. "I nearly stuck myself with the pitchfork when he popped out of the hay over in the barn."

That's where.

"I'm afraid Joel only gets worse, sir," I said.

"'Uncle George,' please. Call me sir at my funeral. That way I can't hear it anyhow."

I nodded again.

"In fact, your brother scared me so good, I sent him to fetch some eggs."

I didn't understand, but that didn't matter. I enjoyed watching the fun in his face as he spoke. My answer came immediately anyway.

From outside came a loud screeching of chickens.

"I wondered how long that would take," Uncle George said. He didn't bother getting up with the rest of us to look out.

Joel was in the yard, running as fast as he could and barely staying a step ahead of a determined, flapping rooster.

"Old Barney don't take kindly to strangers," Uncle George said mildly from the kitchen table.

The rooster chased Joel all the way to the back steps. I knew this vacation was going to be just fine.

CHAPTER 5

"Mike, tell us again we're having fun."

"What's wrong with a little work?" he asked me.

Ralphy snorted. "If this is a *little* work, I'm King Kong."

"And I'm the jet planes who shot him down," I added.

"For once, I have to agree with Ricky," Sarah said. Then stuck her tongue out at me.

We were at the far edge of the farmyard. Looking back at the house, I could see Joel hoeing in the garden with Aunt Edith. That, at least, would keep him out of our way for a while.

The lines of the ranch house stood straight and white against the backdrop of the hills behind it. The house, the garden, the farmyard area, and all the buildings were perched on a small plateau halfway up one side of the valley. Looking the other way, I could see where the road wound its way down the hill to the river at the bottom of the valley and followed it out of sight to the town of Wolf Creek. And everywhere I looked, there was sky. Big, blue sky. Enough to put me in a good mood. Except there was the shed in front of us.

Actually, it was no longer a shed. It was pieces of a shed, squashed by the huge cottonwood tree that had crashed onto its roof during the same storm that had knocked out the telephone line and stranded the two women Joel had rescued with the bus.

"First we have to saw the tree into firewood-sized chunks," Mike said. "Then we have to separate the shed into junk lumber and usable lumber."

"Definitely my idea of a vacation, pal," I said. "When we finish—just for fun—can we dig fence-post holes for the rest of the day?"

"Can I help it if a storm came through the valley three days ago?" he said.

Ralphy's eyes widened. "And what a storm! I thought we were going to get blown off the hillside. Thunder! Lightning! It roared worse than Uncle George looking for his breakfast."

"Did I hear my name?"

Uncle George rounded the corner of the barn on a huge black horse. As usual, he was grinning widely. *Those teeth of his see a lot of sunlight*, I thought.

Uncle George climbed down from his horse and wrapped the reins around a fence post. The horse immediately dropped its head and began grazing at the long grass along the fence.

"It was a wicked storm all right." He lowered his voice to a conspiring whisper. "In fact, folks around here are saying it was the worst one since the storm of the phantom outlaw back in 1950."

"The phantom outlaw!" Ralphy jumped.

"I haven't told you that one yet, have I?" Uncle George replied. He plucked a long green stem of grass and began chewing at the pale yellow part near the base of the blade. "Yup. The storm of the phantom outlaw. It happened about six years after the Second World War. The early 1950s. I'm sixty-three years old now, so back then I was just a little younger than you kids."

I guessed at that age he was probably just like Mike, always playing jokes and looking for fun and trouble.

"This is the way it happened." Uncle George cleared his throat and stared at the sky, gathering his thoughts.

"First of all, there was the bank robbery."

"Bank robbery!" Once again Ralphy jumped.

"Yup. Delilah Abercombe robbed the Wolf Creek Bank the afternoon of the storm."

"A woman bank robber," Sarah said with a shine in her eyes. It was the first time I had seen her enthusiastic.

Uncle George knew he had an interested audience. He leaned back against a fence post and took his time.

"Delilah Abercombe was about twenty at the time, as I recall. Her dad died during the war. She was very pretty. I remember always seeing her in church and admiring her long, long blond hair. The day of the storm, she marched into the bank, pulled a pistol from her purse, and demanded all the money the cashier could find."

"Wow," Sarah sighed.

Uncle George glared at her. "Don't be getting any ideas." He grinned. "Anyway, strange thing was she made them take a bunch of papers from the safe. That's what got her into trouble. She spent too much time waiting for those papers, and the sheriff walked in on the robbery. He took one look at the gun, ran outside, and rounded up a posse."

"No shootout?" Mike sounded disappointed.

"No shootout. Delilah scooped up the papers, hopped on a horse, and got going. It gave her a five-minute head start on the posse. That's all she needed."

The way he was taking his time to tell the story was killing me.

"All she needed for what?" I finally had to ask.

"To get to the Wolf Creek cliffs.

"She made it to the cliffs ten minutes ahead of the posse. And an hour ahead of the storm. You have to understand, there is only one way in or out of that area, and that's where the creek leaves the cliffs. They posted half the men at the entrance and the other half went in. No luck. Delilah Abercombe had vanished. The tragic part is that the storm hit an hour later. The worst storm to hit this century."

"Worse than this week's storm?"

Uncle George nodded. "So fierce that the posse didn't dare spend more time in the cliffs. Those are the steepest, most rugged walls of rock in the area. The terrain is difficult enough in good weather for people on foot. And in that storm . . ."

"She got away, though," Sarah said. "I know she got away. Women can outsmart men any time."

"No way," Mike said. "Just try me. Why—"

"What happened to her?" I asked. Mike shot me a dirty look for interrupting.

"That's just it," Uncle George said. "Nobody knows. She didn't come out. After the storm cleared, they went in to look. They expected to find her dead somewhere. But no sign of her. No sign of her horse. No sign of the bank money."

"Nothing?" Sarah said.

"Nothing. Except for one thing. Ever since that storm, folks have been seeing things in those cliffs. Sometimes on moonlit nights, campers look up and see a horse rider galloping through the cliffs, long hair flowing behind in the wind."

"I-i-impossible," Ralphy said. "R-r-right?"

Uncle George gave a low whistle. "I'd say so, too, except the next day they sometimes find horseshoe tracks. In places impossible for any living horse to climb."

Sarah smirked. "I knew she'd fool everybody."

"You might be right, Sarah," Uncle George said. "Sometimes during the day, people will hear hoofbeats clattering on the rock. But they never see a horse."

He stared at the sky. "And nobody has seen a trace of Delilah Abercombe since the night of the storm. They figure it's her ghost in those cliffs. They call her 'The Phantom Outlaw.'"

Despite the warmth of the sun beating down against us, we all shivered. I shivered more than anyone. Between Mike and Sarah, I knew there was no way we'd get out of visiting those cliffs.

CHAPTER 6

Uncle George stood again. "Well," he said. "Time to get me and Old Black moving. A few head of cattle have been missing ever since the storm. I figure I should be able to find them near water."

"That makes sense," Mike said.

It didn't to me. I hadn't been here for a week already.

"Water?" I asked.

"Yup," Mike said smugly. "This area's been dry for quite some time. In some places, it's almost in drought condition. Naturally, all the livestock will hang out around water holes."

"But this tree fell on the shed because of a storm," Sarah protested.

Uncle George waved away some flies from Old Black's neck. "Funny thing is, that storm dumped too much water on us in too short a time. It just runs off the land into the creeks and washes away. Conditions aren't bad enough around here to start worrying yet, but we could use a long gentle rain to really soak the ground. Until then, cattle will follow their noses to water. And we"—he patted Old Black— "will follow the water to them."

He swung a long leg over the saddle and they trotted out of sight. I hoped to be able to ride like that before the vacation was over.

We worked on the shed for two hours. Aunt Edith stopped by with lemonade and told us that was enough work for anybody.

"The rest of the day is yours," she said. "I'll watch Joel.

Mike and Ralphy know where the horses are. So do some riding if you like, but stay together. The hills are safe, of course, but I'd rather you always had someone around in case of trouble."

"I understand," Mike said gravely.

Aunt Edith laughed. "Mike Andrews, if you think that serious look fools me, think again. Keep an eye on your friends and don't scare them with stories about the hermit Quigley. Because that's all they are. Stories."

"Well, we're off," Mike said.

We were all saddled up and heading out of the barnyard into the hills. I had a red-brown horse called Sheba who seemed friendly enough. Unfortunately, it had to be Sarah who taught me how to saddle it.

It was my first time on a horse. The leather reins were knotted together, and I held them in one hand. Sarah had explained to me that this was the Western style of riding, and that the horse had been trained to respond to neck reining. Swing your hand to the right, she'd said, and the horse responds to the light pressure on its neck to turn that way. Same for the left. This method, she'd said, left ranchers with a free hand to do other things. Like throwing a lasso, for example. I had told her I was more concerned about finding the brakes. Simple, she told me, just pull both the reins back at the same time.

"Sheba," I whispered as we left the barnyard, "be nice to a kid from the city." There were twelve hundred pounds of live muscle below me. In a situation like that, you definitely want to start off as friends.

Horse riding couldn't be that bad, I told myself. Not if Ralphy was riding with such confidence. Of course, he had a small old black horse named Grandma.

Mike's horse was a bay, and, without riding it once, he'd already bragged to Sarah that it was faster than hers. But that's Mike.

Trees, mostly clumps of poplar, filled the little gullies that formed in the sides of the hills. Far below us, towering cottonwoods grew along the sides of the creek, where there was enough water to support them.

The hills themselves were not steep. They stretched along the valley in long, rolling waves of grassy land. The cry of crows reached us, and a slight breeze rippled the top of the grass.

Altogether, with the mountains beyond the far hills rising in a purple haze to meet the sky, it was beautiful. It reminded me of something my dad once tried to teach me about praising God. Church and hymns were one way of doing it, he said. But he also explained that God took great joy in seeing his children receive joy in life. Thinking of it that way made sense; sometimes I had fun watching Joel have fun, especially if it was fun with a gift I had given him. Dad told me that praise can be as simple as realizing God is our gift giver. Enjoying something and knowing God is the source, he had said, is a way of praising, too. So I grinned at the blue sky.

The ride was so relaxing, I wanted to keep it that way. As I rocked up and down to the rhythm of Sheba's walk, I said, "Don't even think about it, Mike. The bank robbery is over fifty years old. And there's no such thing as ghosts."

"How did you guess we were on our way to the cliffs?" Fake amazement filled his face as he sat tall in his saddle beside me.

I said, "What am I? Stupid?"

"Anybody who can lose a brother on a bus..." Sarah broke in from behind us.

All I wanted to say was, "See if *you* could keep up with Joel." Except I never finished the sentence.

My mistake was to turn in the saddle to give Sarah a withering look. I slipped in the saddle, and to keep my balance, I flung my foot back. The heel of my shoe kicked the horse solidly in the ribs.

What I actually said was, "See if you could keep up—" and the rest of it was lost in the explosion of hoofbeats as a keg of dynamite named Sheba blew sky-high because of that simple accidental kick.

The first five seconds of that ride stunned me with adrenaline. I felt my eyebrows shoot straight ahead with the shock of his full-force gallop.

By the time I remembered the way to use the brakes was to pull on the reins, I had already dropped them and was hugging Sheba's neck with both arms and a madman's death grip.

It only made him run harder.

His hooves pounded the ground, and thunder filled my ears. I glanced at the ground and saw only a blur of grass and small bushes and decided I was better off looking straight ahead.

Which was another mistake. I saw a barbed wire fence.

I yelled. Mistake number three. Sheba thought that I was yelling to go faster. So he did.

So I squeezed harder. Which only made my rear end bounce up and down in the saddle like a cannonball going down a set of stairs.

The wind whipped my hair. Over half a ton of hard muscle surged out of control beneath me. And still the fence came closer.

Let go? I wasn't totally crazy.

I did the only sensible thing. I closed my eyes. Suddenly, for a split second, the thunder of Sheba's pounding hooves became a *whooosh*, but before I could decide what had happened, we had landed again. Beyond the fence!

I had survived.

And something strange happened. With the fence behind us, in front was only grassy hillside, and gradually my body began to understand the rhythm of a full gallop.

Forward. Land, leap, and forward. I relaxed and began to enjoy the sureness of a good horse given full rein to run.

Reins!

As I tightened and relaxed with each surge of the gallop, I found the confidence to reach for Sheba's reins.

Once I had the reins in my hand, I sat a little straighter and squeezed with my knees to keep my balance. Then slowly, very slowly, I pulled back on the reins.

Hah! It worked.

Sheba's gallop became a trot. I pulled back harder and the trot became a walk, then a complete stop.

From far behind, I heard the drumming of other hooves. I turned in the saddle—careful this time not to kick Sheba—and saw Sarah in a full gallop about a hundred yards behind, her red hair filled with wind.

"Whoa, Vandy. Whoa," she told her horse as she arrived.

Both our horses sat still beneath us, their sides heaving after the long run.

Sarah had a new look in her eyes. Grudging respect.

I remembered the last thing I had said before Sheba decided to give me a living roller coaster ride.

See if you could keep up.

So I told her, "You're pretty fast on a horse. Not many can stay that close when I feel like testing a horse for speed."

CHAPTER 7

After Mike and Ralphy caught up to us, I remembered a question I had intended to ask as we left the farmyard.

"Who's this Quigem person, Mike?"

"Quigley," he said. "His name is Quigley."

The four of us rode our horses in single file along a well-worn path on the side of the hill. The cliffs were on the close edge of the ranch, and Mike said we had at least ten minutes of riding to get there.

"He's a hermit!" Ralphy said from the rear of the line. "If he catches you on his property, he'll tie you to a tree and leave you there for days!"

"No way," Sarah said.

"Really," Ralphy insisted. "Me and Mike heard that in the store when we went to Wolf Creek with Uncle George and Aunt Edith."

"Mike?" I said.

"That's what they said, all right. Not only that, but he loads an old shotgun full of salt and shoots at anybody, especially kids, he finds on his land."

It sounded like a good enough reason to stay clear of him.

"Plus, he has a vicious black dog," Ralphy said. "Big and mean. They told us it's part wolf. Runs as fast as a horse and has a bite worse than a bear trap. Quigley keeps it chained until he hears someone on his land. Then he lets it loose, and good luck to any trespassers!"

Even Sarah was impressed. "Where does he live?"

"We haven't seen it yet," Mike said. I didn't like the

hey told us his land goes right to the edge of the
operty runs beside Uncle George's, but there's a
eep people out, so at least we can't wander onto

a phantom outlaw and a crazy hermit, the
ike a dream vacation. Especially since those
ere nothing compared to the big one—my brother, Joel.

The trail took us to the bottom of the valley. The creek bed of
Wolf Creek was as wide as I could throw a stone. The water going
through it was barely a trickle. Mike explained that once the spring
runoff from the melting snow in the mountains was finished, the creek
usually shrank a bit. This year, though, because of the dryness, there
was hardly any water at all.

And it was hot as we rode. I mopped my head and decided to be
sure to bring a canteen next time.

There was enough room for the horses to ride along the creek
bed. The banks of the creek were slightly higher than our heads, so
we could see only forward or backward to the next turn of the creek,
but not to the sides.

We were completely protected from any wind, and without a
breeze the air felt crisp against our faces. A high buzzing of insects
made a symphony around us.

The creek bed and the trickle of water disappeared as abruptly as
if we had reached the end of a table. Only after slowly moving closer
to the edge did we see enough to understand. Like a waterfall without
water, the land dropped into a steep gorge where water had worn its
way down over the centuries.

Ralphy whistled. "Limestone formations." Maybe that isn't stan-
dard knowledge for a twelve-year-old, but Ralphy's a computer whiz,
and no fact he recites will ever surprise me.

"Limestone?" Sarah asked.

"Yes," he said. "A very soft type of rock. Water cuts through it
quicker than it does most rock."

She frowned.

Ralphy pointed at the boulders strewn along the steep drop of the gorge. "At one time, those were probably imbedded in limestone. Like marbles held together with glue until water washes it away. What's left are the marbles and whatever they were resting on."

Made sense to me. I mean, I could see the results.

The gorge widened to the size of a football field. Stunted trees and heavy bushes grew haphazardly among the cliffs.

I threw a rock far into the gorge. It took several seconds to land and clatter among the boulders at the bottom.

I could see what Uncle George meant when he said the other end of the cliffs were the only way in or out. On this end, a mountaineer would be lucky to get down using a rope.

"Shhhhh!" Sarah said. "I hear something."

"Sure," Mike said. "A phantom horse?"

The next sound sent shivers crawling into my hair.

It was the shrill whinnying of a horse! From somewhere ahead in the gorge?

"That was our imagination, right?" Ralphy said.

Sheba began to prance nervously. Which made me nervous.

There was silence, except for the whine of insects. Sheba snorted once, then settled down.

"It did sound like a horse," Mike finally said.

"If it wasn't," I said, "it was a good imitation."

Before anyone could reply, we heard another whinny. This time much louder. Then a pounding of hooves. We finally realized the sound was coming from behind us.

Aunt Edith rounded the bend of the creek bed and drew her horse up short of us.

"Am I glad to see you," she said. "I need your help."

What could it be to put so much concern into her strong face?

She took a breath. Drops of sweat lined her forehead. "It's Joel," she continued. "I can't find him anywhere."

Wonderful. It took him less than a day.

"How well can you ride?" Aunt Edith asked me.

I wanted to tell her it was no problem as long as the horse was doing under five miles per hour.

Remembering Sarah, I shrugged instead.

"Ricky can ride fast, Aunt Edith," Sarah said. "Faster than me, even."

"Good," Aunt Edith said. "Ricky, we need to get back as soon as possible. The rest of you follow us, but take your time. I don't like the thought of everyone at a full speed gallop."

She reined her horse around sharply and spurred it back down the creek.

I grinned weakly at Sarah and Mike and Ralphy.

Then I gritted my teeth and tapped Sheba with my heel. Unfortunately, not quite softly enough. Sheba bucked once and shot forward. I closed my eyes.

CHAPTER 8

My watch told me it took seven minutes to get back to
the ranch house. My heart, which thumped faster than
Sheba's hooves, told me it took forever. I was just glad Aunt
Edith knew a way back that didn't need any fence jumping.

Not until I was in the kitchen and far from Sheba's galloping back did I have the luxury of worrying about Joel.

Aunt Edith was very upset. She kept smoothing imagi-
nary hairs back from her face.

"It's okay," I told her. "He always shows up." *And usually
where you least want him,* I added to myself.

"I can't understand it." In her nervousness, she spoke
quickly. "He was with me here in the kitchen one minute. I
turned my back for a second and he was gone."

Something about the kitchen was bugging me. I couldn't
quite place it.

"It was right in the middle of a nice chat," she continued.
Knowing Joel, that meant Aunt Edith was doing all the talking. "I was telling him about some of the things I believed
when I was his age."

Hah! I knew what it was about the kitchen! Joel's teddy
bear was still there.

"I've looked everywhere," Aunt Edith said. "The barn,
the chicken shed, the feed lot. I yelled my lungs out. But no
sign of him. It's been over an hour. I sure pray he's okay."

"Believe me, I know exactly what you feel like," I told
her, thinking of the bus ride. "Fortunately, I've just noticed
something very interesting."

"Yes?" she said hopefully.

I walked to the kitchen table and grabbed Joel's teddy bear.

"I'm sorry," she said. "I don't understand what makes that interesting."

"It's his only weakness," I explained. "When Joel's sleeping, you can march a band through his room or wave a good-smelling hot dog under his nose and he keeps snoring. But wiggle one paw of his teddy bear, and his eyes pop wide open." I grinned.

"Sometimes when I need to get away from him back in Jamesville, I'll throw his teddy bear in the dryer. He stays and watches it right to the end of the cycle."

Aunt Edith still didn't understand.

"What I mean is that it takes a good reason for Joel to leave without his teddy bear. Once we know the reason, we'll be a lot closer to finding him."

"Well," she said uncertainly, "it sounds like a good theory."

Unfortunately, I've had a lot of practice trying to outguess Joel.

"He's got small hands," I thought aloud. "If he left the teddy bear, he probably carried something else, or was thinking of going out there to get something that needed carrying."

Aunt Edith looked at the kitchen table. Her eyes widened and she smacked her forehead. "Maybe both," she said.

This time *I* was puzzled.

"I can tell you one thing that's missing. Something he had to carry out of here," she said. "The saltshaker."

The saltshaker?

She groaned. "And it explains what he might be hoping to carry back. I was telling him an old wives' tale that my mother used to tease me with. Maybe you've heard it before. It's the one that says you can catch a bird by pouring salt on its tail. You don't think he—"

It took me zero time to reply. "Definitely," I said.

Joel loves animals. And they usually love him. He feeds wild squirrels by hand. The Bradleys' German shepherds in Jamesville lick him gently; they kill themselves against their fence whenever Mike or I walk by. I fully expected even Barney the rooster to obediently follow him around like a pet dog before our vacation was over. Everything wild is a pet to him, from mice to snakes, as I have learned the hard way.

The worst part about Joel's disappearance was his stubbornness.

If he believed that salt would get him a bird, he wouldn't quit trying until you dragged him away and tied him down. But, of course, he had to be found first.

Mike, Ralphy, and Sarah walked into the back porch and peered into the kitchen.

"Well," Aunt Edith said slowly, "I guess we'd better start looking for birds."

My first warning of something wrong was a thump that felt like a kick in the pants. My second warning was landing on my stomach and looking straight into the dried mud and scattered straw.

My third warning was a long bleat that sounded too much like a laugh.

We had scattered in all directions on leaving the house. Since I had been here only a day, I wasn't familiar with all of the buildings and fenced yards.

The one I had chosen to cross looked innocent enough. Fence made of wood railings. An area the size of a baseball diamond. A pile of straw in one corner. And a waving in the grass on the other side that might have been Joel.

So I had hopped the fence to take the shortcut straight across. I should have known something would go wrong when I heard a rustling from the pile of straw. But I was so worried about Joel, I ignored it. And the result of my inattention was a nosedive into the dried mud and straw.

I stood up and tried to turn around. Before I could—*thump*—I was knocked down again.

Bleeeaaatt!

What is *it?*

It doesn't take me long to learn things. This time I looked over my shoulder before trying to stand. All I saw was beard. Long white beard. Then a laughing pinched face and long skinny horns curved up and backward.

A billy goat!

Wrong. Two billy goats. Two *big* billy goats. At least four feet high each.

I was ready to consider their actions a personal insult. That, however, did not help me get to my feet.

I tried crawling. The billy goats lowered their heads and moved forward to butt me again. I froze.

They stopped and stared, with big yellow eyes that looked like glazed china. And grins, I was sure, across their faces.

I inched forward. They dropped their heads again. I stopped. They stopped.

Wonderful. I was safe as long as I didn't move. Why is it, every time Joel gets into trouble, I'm the one who suffers?

I lay there, straw jabbing into my nose, as I considered my next move. Could I get up in time to outrun them?

I pushed myself up as quick as I could and—

Thump! Butted in midstride.

This time I stayed on the ground. Both goats bleated at once. *Glad to keep you boys entertained*, I thought.

What to do? Sure, I could make it to the fence eventually, but only after they played pinball with me another dozen times. No, I would lie there until I outthought them. If I couldn't outsmart a couple of dumb billy goats—

A rope landed on my head. A heavy rope that slapped my ears and drove my face farther into the straw.

"I thought it was Joel who needed rescuing," a voice called out.

And here I was thinking life couldn't get worse. It was Sarah's voice.

"I've done some roping back in Wyoming," she said. "Usually I don't miss that bad. I should be able to get them in a couple more tries."

"So who needs your help?" I said, spitting mud. "A fella can't rest wherever he chooses?"

Her next throw looped the rope over the first billy goat's horns. From where my face was buried sideways, I could see her tying her end of the rope to the fence.

"That's one of them," she called. "Think you can outrun the other? Or do I need to find some more rope?"

With one billy goat out of commission, I could at least make it to my feet. Which I did.

I walked with as much dignity as possible to the fence. Only then did I brush myself off.

By the time I got there, Sarah had walked away.

Why is that girl so antisocial?

CHAPTER 9

I began to worry when my original fail-safe method—using Joel's teddy bear as bait—didn't work.

Joel disappears frequently, almost as many times as he suddenly appears and gives you a heart attack. But he never ignores his teddy bear.

The way we get around that in Jamesville is by taking the teddy bear hostage. Since Joel thinks if his teddy bear's eyes are covered, nobody can see it, it's easy to find. The idea is to kidnap his teddy bear early in the day, and when you want Joel to appear, you simply threaten, very loudly, to take the stuffing out. Then, like magic, Joel will somehow be in front of you, staring at you with mournful eyes.

This time, no matter how much abuse we promised the teddy bear at the top of our lungs, Joel remained in his normal state—gone.

Where could he be?

We had already covered all four corners of the farmyard and were considering a move to widen the search area by scouring the countryside on horseback.

Aunt Edith decided she would take one final look through the house. Mike, Ralphy, Sarah, and I leaned against the fence that surrounded the hay shed. On the other side of the fence, a dozen fat and lazy cows munched on feed in the shade of the huge shed.

"Does he disappear often?" Sarah asked. So far, she had not said anything to Mike or Ralphy about the billy goats. Maybe I could be friends after all.

I felt like laughing hysterically.

"All too often," Mike said. "Joel is terrifying."

Sarah raised her eyebrows to hear someone like Mike admit fear of a six-year-old kid.

"Aaaack!" Ralphy suddenly jumped and pulled his hand violently away from the wood railing. He held his hand as far away from his body as possible and shook it frantically.

"Are you okay?" I asked.

"Yuck," he said. "I'm okay, but this sure is gross."

He showed us the palm of his hand. A fresh green-and-white bird dropping was smeared across the skin where he had leaned on his hand against the fence.

The hazards of country living.

"Pigeons," Ralphy said. The disgust in his voice sent Mike into hoots of laughter.

"Very funny, Mike." Ralphy sniffed. "See if you'd like it."

Mike only laughed harder.

As the dropping on his hand showed, Ralphy is not a lucky person. But the next second finally rewarded him for all his bad luck. It was as if Ralphy had trained the king of pigeon bombers.

Because just as Mike doubled over in laughter—*splat*—a huge dropping fell from the sky and creamed the back of his neck.

I looked up in time to see the culprit speeding overhead toward the main barn.

"Do *you* like it, Mike? Do *you* like it?" Ralphy howled with laughter. Then he proved how unlucky he really is.

His laughter drove him to his knees in helpless, stomach-clutching spasms. *Splurt.* Deep in the clump of grass was hidden a fresh horse pie. Ralphy's laughter instantly changed to a look of horror, and when he stood, he stared mutely at the dark clumped balls that fell to the ground from his pants leg.

Mike was wiping the back of his neck in stunned disbelief.

Sarah was giggling in hiccups and holding the fence to keep from falling. Ralphy was moaning.

And I should have been killing myself in laughter at their reactions.

Instead, I was staring at the top of the barn. As if it were a train station, pigeons were coming and going out of a small opening on the second story every few seconds.

Put yourself in Joel's shoes, I told myself. *You're six years old and you want to catch a bird. You step outside and see birds going in and out of the barn. Where would you go?*

The answer was so obvious, I wanted to kick myself.

"I know where Joel is," I said.

Nobody listened.

"I know where Joel is." This time louder.

Still nothing.

I screamed, "I know where Joel is!"

It finally cut through Sarah's laughter and the horrified looks Mike and Ralphy were exchanging.

Between gasps, Sarah said, "Where?"

"Where the birds are." I pointed at the barn. "There, on the second story."

"It's called a hayloft," Sarah said.

"Whatever. I'm sure he's there."

"I checked there twice," Ralphy said. He stared at his dirty knee and looked ready to cry.

"Did you check every square inch of the hayloft?"

"Well, I shouted up the ladder. . . ."

"There you go. He's there."

"You go get him, then," Mike said, gingerly touching his neck. "I need to get some tissue."

"Don't worry about the pigeon." I grinned. "It's long gone by now."

"Hah, hah." Mike scowled at me and began walking back to the house. He stayed in a hunched-over position, scared to have anything trickle down his neck onto his back. Ralphy followed, hopping on one leg and shaking the other.

That left Sarah and me to find Joel.

The barn was cool and had a comforting smell of sweet hay. It was dark, and my eyes took a couple minutes to adjust.

Sarah stepped boldly forward. As I followed, I began to finally see the interior. We were walking down a main aisle with empty square stalls on both sides, with a floor of chipped concrete. Above us, the wide planks of ceiling showed gaps with hay and straw sticking down.

"They mostly use this for livestock in the winter," Sarah said. "And the hayloft above us stores, of course, hay."

I was trying to get used to having a girl lecture me when she stopped short.

"Joel!" she shouted.

"I wouldn't bother," I said. "When he wants to stay gone, yelling only warns him. When he wants to appear, he does it whether you want it or not."

We walked farther. Sarah pointed to nailed slats of wood that made a ladder up the side of the barn's interior. "That's the way up," she said.

There was a trapdoor opening through the ceiling. It was a tall ladder. I could see why Ralphy had declined to climb it.

I, however, didn't have any choice. If Joel weren't up there, we would have no idea where to look next. And a missing brother is a serious thing.

We climbed. I went first and helped Sarah get through the opening.

The air was dusty, but the beam of sunlight that poured into the loft still gave a nice gleam from Sarah's red hair. Piles of hay were scattered everywhere.

No Joel.

Pigeons cooed in low warbles. Then there was another noise, a rustling in the hay.

Sarah looked at me.

"Mice?" she guessed.

I shook my head no.

We crept forward in the dimness of the hayloft. Then we saw Joel in the far corner, half hidden by a pile of hay.

"There you are!" Sarah said.

Joel didn't move. Which at first glance froze me with a sudden fear. Joel, my ghostly kid brother, unable to move? *What is wrong?*

I put a warning hand out to slow down Sarah. Maybe Joel was stuck where the floor of the hayloft had rotted, and maybe all of us would break through if we put too much weight in one area. Or maybe a piece of farm equipment buried in the hay had snapped shut, holding him prisoner while all of us looked for him. Or maybe—

I groaned. *Only Joel,* I told myself.

Only Joel would be able to catch them in the first place. And only Joel would be too stubborn to let them go.

Sarah didn't believe her eyes. But I had been living with Joel long enough to accept the impossible.

Joel was sitting in the hay, with his back to the wall. Trapped gently between his legs was a pigeon, head strained high and eyes darting from side to side. He had another pigeon pinned to the floor with his right hand. And another pinned to the floor with his left hand. He'd probably been holding them like that for an hour.

He smiled shyly at us. "Think Mom will like this? Maybe we'll start a zoo, okay?"

I sighed. Getting Joel to stand up and let go of the pigeons would break his heart.

CHAPTER 10

By the time supper was ready, my body had begun to remember the billy goats. I could barely sit down from the pain of the bruises.

But no one noticed. Joel was already at the table, eyes dreamily focused outside on the potential zoo he had discovered. Ralphy kept rubbing his hands together, as if he were washing them under the tap. Mike's head twitched.

Overshadowing all of that was the worry that showed plainly on Uncle George's face.

"No luck with the missing cattle?" Aunt Edith asked.

"Worse," Uncle George said. "Another one is gone. And when I called around to see if the neighbors have seen them, most of them said they were missing cattle, too."

Suddenly the worry on his face vanished as he remembered something else. He grinned widely, bunching the tanned wrinkles around his eyes. "Which one of you varmints roped Billy One by the horns and left him tied to the fence?"

I was in the middle of scooping mashed potatoes on my plate and my hand froze in midair.

Sarah and I forgot all about the goat!

Sarah blushed. "I did," she said.

"If you ever took roping lessons," Uncle George told her, grin still growing, "you forgot the difference between cattle and goats. Cows are bigger and their horns go to the sides, not straight up. And you're supposed to rope them on the range, not in a pen where they can't get away."

I broke in. "It's my fault," I said. "She was, uh, rescuing me."

Much as I didn't want it known, I explained how stupid I had been.

Uncle George started laughing so hard the table shook.

"Mike," he roared, "you didn't warn your friends about Billy One and Billy Two?"

Mike studied his fingernails.

"Of course not," Uncle George said. "Because then you'd have to explain how they trapped you in there for a whole afternoon last summer. How you were scared to move for five hours!"

That made my soreness feel a lot better.

Uncle George sobered quickly. "It doesn't do much good to know how to rope your cattle," he said thoughtfully. "Not if rustlers are beating you to it."

Aunt Edith gasped. "Rustlers?"

"That's what it sounds like." The worry on his face returned.

We spent the next two days finishing the work on the destroyed shed in the mornings and riding horses in the afternoon. Both afternoons, though, Aunt Edith helped Uncle George with some fencing repairs, so we had to watch Joel.

That meant our freedom was restricted. We did not get back to the Wolf Creek cliffs. We convinced ourselves the horse we had heard the first afternoon was Aunt Edith's and that the echoes among the cliffs had fooled us into thinking the sound came from in front of us, instead of behind.

Sarah spent time teaching all of us more riding tricks, and I became comfortable enough with Sheba so that I didn't mind when Joel sat behind me in the saddle as we crossed the hills. Sarah was never quite sure about my horse riding. Thanks to my first ride on Sheba, Sarah half suspected I was an expert now pretending to be learning. Not that I was in a hurry to let her discover the truth.

My only complaint was Aunt Edith's dumb cat.

Every morning I woke up with a custom-made, living, breathing, and lazy fur coat on my face. Why couldn't the stupid cat use someone else for a bed?

On Saturday morning, after I had knocked the cat off my face and finished breakfast, Aunt Edith stopped by as Mike and I washed the dishes.

"On Saturdays Uncle George and I go into Wolf Creek for shopping. Anybody interested in joining us?"

"Can we handcuff Joel?" Mike asked.

Nobody answered. I made sure we had his teddy bear.

It took about twenty minutes of driving along the gravel road from the ranch to get to the town of Wolf Creek. Where the land flattened out in the valley just before reaching town, I saw what looked like huge iron seesaws.

"Oil pumps," Uncle George explained. "At one time they brought up a fortune in crude oil. They dried up about ten years ago. It costs more to tear them out than it does to leave them in. But I think they're ugly, and I've told Mr. Keyster that myself many times."

"He's another farmer?" I asked.

"Nope. The banker. Nice enough guy. The bank's held that land ever since I was a kid. You'd think with the money they made from that oil, they could afford to haul those old pumps away."

That was all Uncle George said on the subject. As he finished speaking, we entered the town of Wolf Creek.

All I had seen of it before was the parking lot of the truck stop where the bus had dropped us off at night. In daylight, it seemed much smaller. It made my hometown of Jamesville look like New York. One main street ran through the center. Along it, for three blocks, stood the small buildings that held the local businesses. A few blocks on each side held smaller streets with houses. It had one school, two churches, and a baseball diamond. The truck stop was on the exit road that led back to Interstate 15.

Still, I liked it. The buildings were not run down like the way you imagine old western towns from cowboy movies. Most of them had fresh paint, and there were potted flowers set along the sidewalks.

Uncle George parked the truck in front of the local bank.

"So that's the bank that was robbed by Delilah Abercombe," Sarah stated.

Uncle George nodded. "Now, don't you get any ideas."

"I forgot my gun," she said.

It was hard to tell whether she was serious.

She said she had something she wanted to see, and she took Joel and Ralphy with her. Uncle George and Aunt Edith took Mike and me to the general store.

It was small and crowded, with fading tile floors and high shelves crammed with cans and boxes. In the front, however, by the cash register, there was enough space for a couple of cane chairs and a small coffee table with magazines.

A man in coveralls was there relaxing when we came into the store.

"Howdy, Eb," Aunt Edith said.

He took off his dusty baseball cap, groaned getting to his feet, and nodded. "Edith, George. Young'uns. How are you this fine day?"

Eb was bald and had a thick blond beard. He looked older than Uncle George, and with the way he groaned sitting down again, he sounded older, too.

He didn't wait to see how we were this fine day. "My joints hurt. Seem to be drying out in this heat wave," he said. "Any luck with them missing cattle, George? I hear tell your neighbors have the same problem."

"Yes—" Uncle George began.

"It only makes sense," Eb interrupted. "You all have one neighbor in common, you know. Quigley Spears. And I heard he ain't the best person to have living next doors."

"Now, Eb," Aunt Edith began. "Quigley may not be the friendli—"

Eb ignored her, too. "Plain as a train accident, Quigley's the one taking your cattle. Why, from the day he moved onto that land, I heard weird things been happening. There oughta be a law against hermits. That's what I figure. 'Course, I got better things to worry about. My joints are treating me cruel. Every time I go to stock these shelves, it hurts more. Why—"

"Tea," I said.

"What's that!" Eb obviously didn't like being interrupted.

"Tea. You know, the stuff you put in boiling water and drink. I heard if you fill a tub with hot water, add two dozen tea bags, and soak in it for a couple hours it really helps."

Eb scratched his beard. "Tea?"

I nodded. "I heard it's the chemicals that make the water brown that do it. Absorbic acid, or some name like that. Seeps through the skin and relaxes joints."

"Makes sense to me," Eb said after scratching his chin thoughtfully. "Strong tea is a potent brew. Why don't you folks go on ahead and finish your shopping. My wife will be right out to take care of you."

For a big, fat man, he left the chair in a hurry. It didn't seem his joints were bothering him then.

Aunt Edith laughed. "He'll do anything not to work."

I noticed Mike's face staring at me strangely. "Where exactly did you hear this theory on tea?" he asked.

"Just as I was saying it." I grinned. "You heard it, too, didn't you?"

Aunt Edith groaned. "Ricky, you can't do things like that."

"But wasn't he telling us what he'd heard about Quigley?"

"I declare!" a voice boomed through a doorway near the back of the store. "Which of you puppies told ol' Eb about a tea bath?"

CHAPTER 11

I winced. The voice belonged to a lady bigger than Eb and twice as loud. She closed in on us like a hungry linebacker.

"I did," I admitted reluctantly.

"Now you're in for it," Aunt Edith whispered. "That's Eb's wife, Elma. Saves me having to give you a lecture."

The big lady came over and pumped my hand. "Congratulations, son. Ol' Eb thought he knew it all. You just put a whopper past him that makes him look sillier than a newborn goose. I don't even mind having to tend the store to see him be so foolish."

She chortled until she coughed. "Yup. He's setting there right now, steeping in a hot tub and twenty-four bags of tea. Folks aren't gonna let him forget this one."

She waved a massive arm at us. "You two have a couple of chocolate bars," she said to Mike and me. "Then skedaddle. Gossip ain't no fun with young folks around."

As we left the store to explore the town, I decided to ask Mike about something that had been bothering me for a few days.

"Your cousin always seems to be in a bad mood. Is it something I did, or we did, or what?"

Mike sighed. "I don't know her that well. After all, she's from Wyoming, so I don't see her that often. Last year she was fine. Fun, happy, always trying to find trouble. This summer . . . I guess it's because her dad died."

"That's right," I said. "Aunt Edith told me it was a farming accident last fall. Sarah took it hard."

Mike nodded. "And Sarah won't talk about it. Not with me, not with Aunt Edith or Uncle George. It's like something is festering."

"So we leave her alone?"

Before Mike could reply, Sarah nearly bumped into us as she ran out of the building beside us. In a window a sign spelled out WOLF CREEK GAZETTE.

"I found something interesting!" she said, short on breath, and then she stopped. "Where's Ralphy and Joel?"

I groaned. "You didn't let them wait out here, did you?"

"I just wanted to do a little research."

Mike butted in. "And you actually expected them to stay?"

"But Ralphy—" she started.

"—has got an attention span shorter than Joel's," I said.

"That kid," she said. "And to think I wanted them both for my next research."

"School project?" Mike teased.

"No," she snapped. "Reward."

That got our attention.

"No one ever solved that bank robbery," she said. "No one ever saw Delilah Abercombe again. I looked through the *Gazette*'s files. There's still a reward if it's solved. Ten thousand dollars."

"Fat chance," Mike said.

"Let her talk, Mike," I said.

She unthawed her face to smile. Even that tiny bit of a smile changed her face completely.

She became serious quickly. "Think, guys. What was strange about the story Uncle George told us?"

"That a woman outsmarted the men," Mike said. For which he received a scowl that did a thunderstorm justice.

I snapped my fingers. "Not quite, Mike. Although that was my second guess." I rushed on before Sarah could react. "The strange part was those papers. Uncle George said she was waiting and waiting at the safe. Why would a bank robber waste precious time waiting for some stupid papers? She knew the sheriff had seen her. Why not—"

"—take the money and run," Sarah finished for me.

"Good question." Mike nodded at people passing us on the sidewalk. Most of them smiled politely at the way he was dressed. I get so used to his Hawaiian shirts, I forget how distracting they can be.

"So what research do you have planned next?"

"Let me guess," I said. "The bank?"

"Right. None of the articles reported exactly what those papers were. Maybe someone at the bank can tell us. I was going to take Ralphy and Joel, change dollar bills into quarters for video games, and ask a few questions at the same time."

"Take us instead." I paused. Sarah must have forgotten her hostage inside the newspaper office. "And remember the teddy bear. That way we can find Joel when we're finished."

Sarah ducked back inside and sheepishly returned with the teddy bear. I knew from experience how silly she probably felt about it, so I carried it for her.

The bank was so small, it had only one teller's window. On one wall there was a framed photograph of young soldiers posing stiffly. An old man called out from behind the teller's window.

He had gray hair combed sideways across the top of his head, like he was trying to cover a bald spot. His suit jacket was dark blue and flecked with dandruff. And he had gleaming, smooth false teeth. He must have been in his eighties.

"Hello. Come in to open an account?"

"Uh, we need some change," Mike said.

"How much?"

Sarah put a five-dollar bill on the counter. "Quarters, please. For video games."

"Waste of good money," he grunted.

While he was counting, Sarah hinted, "Nice day if it doesn't storm."

He nodded, concentrating on the count of quarters. I noticed how crisply his white shirt had been ironed. At the end of his sleeves, huge polished cuff links filled the buttonholes.

"What are those cuff links made of, Mr. Keyster?" I asked.

"Garnets." The old banker smiled slightly and nodded, which meant I had guessed his name right. So *he* was the person who didn't mind spoiling the view with rusting oil pumps.

"There you are." He pushed the quarters across the counter.

"My uncle told us about the bank robbery the afternoon of the big storm over fifty years ago," Sarah said.

"Your uncle?"

"George Andrews."

"Oh," he said. "You're the kids staying there."

We nodded.

"Well," Mr. Keyster said, "you know how people like to tell stories. I'm sure you've already heard what they've made up about the phantom outlaw."

Sarah's eyes grew bright. "Isn't she something?"

Mr. Keyster frowned. "I don't think so. I'm sorry to say that Delilah deserved what she got. I was behind this exact counter the day she robbed us. And it was not fun, let me tell you."

"'What she got'?" Sarah asked. "I thought she disappeared."

"Hah. Only if you believe those stories. I'm sure she was washed away in the storm."

"But the creek is so small," I said.

"Son," Mr. Keyster said, "in a big storm that creek becomes a river. It's so bad, every time that happens the path of that creek bed changes completely. You can believe in a phantom if you like, but the truth is, she was lost in the storm."

"And all that money," Sarah said. "And the papers."

Mr. Keyster's eyes widened slightly. Or it might have been my imagination. "It was the money that mattered," he said. "We replaced the property deeds almost right away."

"Property deeds?"

"Delilah had no idea, of course," Mr. Keyster stated. "But she took property that was worthless. She was a silly young woman who thought the safe held stock certificates and such."

A man entered the bank.

"Well, she certainly paid the price for her crime," Mr. Keyster finished. Then he smiled without warmth. "I have another customer."

We left slowly. It didn't take long to find Ralphy and Joel. They were already at the arcade.

Ralphy, our computer genius, had already racked up 200,000 points on Pac-Man. That's how small the town was. The whole arcade consisted of one Pac-Man machine.

Mike said, "When you're finished, Ralphy, I'll bet you a Coke that Joel can put the high score of the day on there."

Ralphy ignored him until he ran the score to 300,000. "Nothing's going to read higher on the machine than that."

"That means you'll take the bet? I still say Joel can now put the high score of the day on the screen."

"Make it two Cokes," Ralphy said. "I'll even pay for Joel's game."

Joel leaned eagerly over the flashing dots. I had never seen him score more than 200 points. He loves watching Pac-Man so much, he forgets to move his man.

How is Mike going to win this *bet?*

We found out immediately.

Mike simply unplugged the machine and plugged it back in again. Ralphy's high score erased as the screen died, and the new score sat at zero.

Mike dropped a quarter into the coin slot.

"Fire away," he said. Joel's first point made it the highest score showing.

"Hasn't anyone told you, Ralphy?" Mike said and whistled tunelessly for a few seconds. "It's not nice to gamble."

CHAPTER 12

"I cannot believe you're remotely serious about this," I told Mike. "It's midnight, and you expect us to walk to the cliffs and back."

Our time in town had gone quickly. Then we had enjoyed the afternoon at the ranch, followed by a huge supper and a baseball game on television before all going to bed early.

Except now Mike stood in front of me outside of the farmhouse. Even in the moonlight, the crazy patterns on his shirt were clear. He also had a knapsack on his back.

"We're standing out here, aren't we?" he demanded. "You've got a flashlight and a baseball bat, don't you? So what's hard to believe about this?"

"For starts, that you convinced Ralphy to come along."

"He called me a chicken," Ralphy said resentfully.

I snorted. "But you *are* a chicken."

"I know. But he was going to tell Sarah."

Well, that explained that. Nobody wants a girl to know he's chicken.

I was out here shivering in the moonlight near the main barn because a pebble had hit my window. No sooner had I opened it to look out than another pebble had bounced off my forehead.

Mike, naturally.

When I had gone outside to yell at him for waking me up, he shined a flashlight into my eyeballs from two feet away and told me to carry the baseball bat. In case of coyotes, he had explained.

Wonderful.

Then he told me if I was going to be grumpy about it, maybe he would invite Sarah instead. She seemed quite smart and might even be pretty good at solving mysteries, he had hinted.

And that explained my being there.

As we walked across the hills to the cliffs, I thought of how nice it would be to have a dog with us. One that was all nose for smelling danger and all teeth for fighting it. Like Scooby-Doo, only smarter and meaner.

The sad part was that Aunt Edith and Uncle George had had a dog. But it had died of old age just before the summer started, and—as Aunt Edith explained it—they didn't have the heart to replace it.

So instead of a faithful dog, I had Ralphy huddling so close he bumped into me every two steps and Mike thinking out loud.

"When the horses go slow, it's a fifteen-minute ride to the cliffs. If we walk fast enough, we can be there in half an hour. Uncle George said the chances of seeing bear in this country are remote, so don't worry."

Ralphy slammed into me. "Bear?"

"Forget I even mentioned it," Mike said. "Plenty of coyotes, though, but apparently they don't attack people."

He added cheerfully, "At least not at night."

Any more of this and I would be carrying Ralphy.

"Look, Mike," I said after pushing Ralphy away, "what exactly do you expect to get out of this excursion?"

"I don't know," he said. "But if there's anything at all to this legend of the phantom outlaw, you'd expect to find out on a night like tonight."

Unfortunately, he had a point. The moon was even brighter than the night Joel and I traveled to Wolf Creek by bus. It must be the clear Montana air, I thought. And the lack of city lights to dim it. The light made everything pretty in a ghostly way, and the stillness of the cool air and the cast of the shadows across the hill almost made the craziness of our trip worthwhile.

There was a faint crunch in the grass behind us. Ralphy and I spun around, and we didn't see anything. We agreed to agree it had been nothing. The moon made the hills around us almost gray, and we were able to see quite far.

I wanted to keep it that way.

"Mike," I said, "when we get to the creek, we're not going to travel in the gully. We'll follow the top edge of the banks."

"Why?"

"Because we can see farther from up top than down in the creek bed. And if anything happens, I'd much rather run than use a baseball bat."

"No sense of adventure," Mike grumbled.

Mike's estimate of time was accurate. It was half an hour past midnight when we arrived at the cliffs. Twice more Ralphy and I thought we heard something move in the grass, but both times we managed to convince ourselves it was our imagination.

"Make yourselves comfortable, boys," Mike announced. "We'll just sit here awhile and wait for the phantom. Anybody for chocolate chip cookies and milk?"

He opened his knapsack. I handed the baseball bat to Ralphy. We all leaned against a ledge of rock and surveyed the gorge below us. In the sharpness of the moonlight, the jumble of boulders looked more helter-skelter than it did in the daytime. And more scary. *The shadows behind those rocks could hide nearly anything.*

To get my mind off the scariness, I asked, "How old are those stars, Ralphy?"

He giggled.

"What?" I said. "That's not a dumb question."

"Let me put it this way," he said. "See that star there?"

"Yeah."

"The light we're seeing right now left that star at least a thousand years ago."

"Explain that," I said, glad for the distraction.

"Light travels at 186,000 miles per second," Ralphy said. "If you flick a light switch in your house, the bulb seems to turn on instantly because it's only across the room."

His voice started sounding dreamy, and I knew Ralphy's mind was inside his books or his computer. "But the moon's a quarter million miles away, so the light reflected from it takes over a second to get here. The sun is ninety-three million miles away; its light takes about seven minutes. That star—" he paused for effect "—is so far away that its light has traveled a thousand years to get this far."

"Wow," Mike said.

"It is fascinating, isn't it," Ralphy agreed.

"No," Mike pointed out. "'Wow' that you know so much garbage. Why don't you give me the win-loss record of the New York Yankees over the last ten seasons, or other useful stuff like that."

"Very funny, Mike. You never know when scientific information will help." It would save our lives before the summer was over, but we didn't know it then.

I ignored both of them and stared at the sky. It was neat to think of the vastness of God's universe. Some of the starlight hitting my eyes just now had begun its journey in the days of King Arthur and Merlin. Or earlier. When the pharaohs ruled Egypt maybe.

Our silence was comfortable for the next few minutes as all of us were lost in our thoughts. Then Mike began restlessly strumming his fingers on the empty cookie package. Or so I thought.

"You're getting pretty good at that, Mike," I said. In school sometimes, we strum our fingers on the desks and see who can do it the fastest, loudest, and longest.

"Pretty good at what?"

"You know. Strumming with your fingers."

"Uh-oh," he said. "I thought that was you strumming on the flash-light."

"Knock it off, guys," Ralphy warned. "You know I throw up if I get too scared."

There was nothing to knock off. The strumming got louder, and suddenly all of us knew one thing. *It was a horse.*

We pushed ourselves into the shadow of the rock.

"Don't get too scared, Ralphy," Mike pleaded. "There's not much room here."

"Shhh!"

Then we saw it!

Across the gorge, outlined sharply against the moon, we saw a rider on a horse. Even from that distance, we could see long hair flowing back from the rider as she moved at full gallop!

"Why did I eat so many cookies?" Ralphy moaned.

The horse and rider faded into shadows. Then the drumming of hooves stopped. There was a long silence, and then we heard a clattering as the horse began to pick its way down into the gorge.

"No horse can do that," I whispered. "Those cliffs are too steep."

"That horse can," Mike hissed in return. "And it sounds like it's headed this way."

Too late. I was talking to emptiness. They'd already left.

By the time I caught up with Ralphy and Mike, the comforting silhouettes of the ranch buildings were clearly in sight.

CHAPTER 13

"Do *you* want to tell Uncle George or Aunt Edith you saw a ghost outlaw last night?" I asked. "They'll be more interested in why you were out there in the first place."

It was late Sunday morning and we had all returned from church services in the town of Wolf Creek. It felt good to be in blue jeans and a T-shirt after the dumb suit I had worn to church. I was happy to be able to breathe without a tie jamming my Adam's apple so bad it had almost become Adam's applesauce.

Mike and Ralphy and I were leaning against the main barn, chewing on long pieces of grass, just like real cowboys. Not that I think grass tastes great.

"They didn't specifically forbid us to go there," Mike pointed out hopefully.

I groaned. "Just like they don't specifically forbid you to bang your head against boulders or specifically forbid you to take money out of the collection plate in church."

"What you're saying is that we can't use my argument."

"Right, Mike."

He sighed. "It seemed like a good idea at the time. I'll tell them and take the blame."

"Not alone," Ralphy said. "We were there, too."

"So was I," Sarah said as she stepped out from behind the corner of the barn. "Except you morons forgot to invite me."

Sarah was carrying the baseball bat, flashlight, and knapsack. The stuff we had left behind in our run of panic the night before.

"Interested in these?" she asked with a smirk.

Wonderful.

"And don't worry about Uncle George and Aunt Edith finding out," she added. "They were the ones who woke me to follow you guys. By the way, lunch is ready."

Sarah spoke first in the farmyard after lunch. "Okay, guys. You promised not to go on any more night excursions. But you didn't promise to stay away from Quigley."

"What? You're as bad as Mike!"

"Please, Ricky," he cut in. "Show some respect."

"I don't want to go." Ralphy's voice quavered. He was still rattled about seeing a phantom outlaw.

"It's daytime," Sarah insisted. "It's a quiet Sunday afternoon. Uncle George and Aunt Edith won't mind if we go for a simple little horse ride."

"Right," I said. "To a hermit who shoots kids with salt from his shotgun. To a hermit who ties people to trees."

"We won't trespass and sneak around," Sarah promised. "We'll ride straight to his house and ask him if he has seen the phantom outlaw lately. And on the way we'll keep our eyes skinned for any signs of stolen cattle. Just think, if we can prove he's the rustler, we'll be heroes."

"No. No, no, no," Ralphy said.

Lunch had not been the disaster I feared. Uncle George had chuckled about the way Sarah had managed to follow us without getting caught. Aunt Edith had made us promise not to sneak out at night without permission. And all of us had talked excitedly about the phantom outlaw.

Was it real? Or was it a person? But how to explain the horse climbing down the cliffs? All Aunt Edith and Uncle George could tell us was that the description matched exactly what people had been seeing for years.

"So far," Uncle George had warned us between gulps of mashed potato, "this outlaw character hasn't hurt anyone. Don't become the first. Until she or it has been figured out, you guys cool it around those cliffs."

A warning I was happy to accept.

I also would have been happy to leave the rustling mystery alone. Not Sarah.

"No, no, no," Ralphy repeated. "We shouldn't do this."

She turned to Ralphy as we ambled through the farmyard.

"Fine, Ralphy. If you don't want to come along, you stay here and keep an eye on Joel." She tossed her hair with a disdainful shake of her head. "The rest of us will have fun without you."

An afternoon with Joel or an afternoon with a frightening hermit. Not an easy decision.

Ralphy chose the hermit. But then Joel chose us by following as we went to saddle our horses.

I sighed and boosted Joel and his teddy bear onto Sheba's back. He tucked the bear into the front of his shirt, then wrapped his arms around my stomach, and we trotted past the main barn into the hills. I tried to blame the fluttering in my stomach on the bouncing of the horse.

As we rode, I mentally reviewed the last few days.

Someone—the people in this area were sure—had been stealing livestock. Elma, the big lady at the store, had told Aunt Edith and Uncle George that all of the neighbors surrounding Quigley's land were missing cattle.

So what were we going to do, I thought, especially if we did find some stolen cattle on his property? A few kids against a crazy hermit armed with a shotgun? *Sure.* This wasn't the movies, where we were guaranteed to win.

And even if that worked out fine—which seemed doubtful—what about that phantom outlaw? It was enough to give me shivers, even in the heat of the sun.

The strange part was that the hills around us looked so open and friendly that it was hard to believe anything sinister could happen.

I changed my mind in a hurry as we reached the edge of Quigley's property.

WARNING! ELECTRIC FENCE!

We stopped our horses a healthy distance away.

"Well, that's too bad," Ralphy said. "We'll have to turn around. Maybe we can play croquet in Aunt Edith's front yard."

"Excellent idea," I said. "Croquet is a real fun—"

"There's a gate farther along that's not electric," Mike said. "Last summer I went past it a few times."

Sarah turned her horse and began following the fence.

"Thanks, Mike," I said, not meaning it.

"No problem." He grinned. "I was dying to see his place last summer, but I never had a good reason to go there."

"You mean last summer you were alone and afraid to go by yourself," I said. "You didn't have friends with you to get shot at or chomped on by a dog."

"Something like that."

"Dog?" Joel piped up from behind me. "Where's a dog?"

It was going to be a long day.

CHAPTER  14

The road beyond the gate was little more than a trail of dried mud. Grass grew high between deep wheel ruts. The road turned and disappeared past a pile of huge boulders. I wanted to turn and disappear in the other direction.

No such luck.

After opening the gate, Sarah and Mike looked at each other, waiting, I think, to see if the other person would chicken out. Then each of them clamped their jaws tight with stubbornness and, side by side, urged their horses straight ahead.

I shrugged and Ralphy quivered; then we followed.

Joel said, "Be nice to see a puppy here, too."

When we rounded the bend, the dried mud road dropped steeply into a tree-filled ravine. Backed into the hill of the ravine, barely forty feet away, stood a small wood shack with a chimney and rickety wood porch.

Quigley's place!

Sarah's horse kicked loose a stone, and its clattering echoed into the ravine.

That's all it took. From what seemed like nowhere, a low, menacing growl rumbled through the hot, still air. Then a rattling of a chain. I saw movement, and at first I thought it was the entire black shadow of the porch.

Wrong, Ricky Kidd, I told myself. The big black thing stood and showed four legs.

All four of our horses stopped in respect.

"Tell me that's an optical illusion," Mike said fearfully.

"Sure, Mike, it's an optical illusion. And McDonald's doesn't sell hamburgers," I replied.

Sarah breathed, "That dog's the size of a horse."

At the sound of our voices, the growl, impossible enough, grew deeper.

"Maybe we could ride it," Joel suggested.

"Ralphy was saying something about a croquet game," Sarah said nervously. "I think it's a great idea. Besides, it doesn't seem like anyone is home. Right, guys?"

"Right," Mike said. "I don't care how big that chain is around the dog's neck. If he decides to chase us, he'll drag the entire house with him."

Mike spun his horse around. That startled Sheba, my horse, into a quick shuffle.

Joel had one arm out as he pointed in fascination at Quigley's dog. To keep his balance, he clutched at me. His teddy bear fell from his shirt to the ground and began rolling toward Quigley's shack.

Before I could react, Joel hopped off the horse and ran after the bear. The steepness of the road sent the bear tumbling ahead, almost to the dog's monstrous paws.

The dog bent its broad dark head in one quick movement and snatched the teddy bear between its jaws. Its growl became thunder!

"Joel!" I hissed.

Too late. My voice was not enough to stop his determined march. He was already there.

If I had had time to think, I probably would have stayed in the saddle. But my fear for Joel spun me out of the saddle and to the ground before I could stop myself.

Time slowed to a crawl. Mike, Ralphy, and Sarah watched helplessly.

A rock. A stick. Anything to rescue my kid brother.

Too late again. Joel stopped briefly in front of the beast, already in reach of those monstrous teeth. The top of Joel's head was barely as high as the dog's massive jaw.

They say the worst thing to show an animal is fear. And with the terror racing through my veins, anywhere near the brute I would have been hamburger within seconds.

Joel, however, didn't let the loud growling slow him for an instant.

"Thank you," he said, then plucked the bear from the dog's jaws.

Can you attribute human expressions to animal faces? If so, the dog's eyes and mouth were saying, "Huh?"

Worse, Joel began petting its head. It was so startled, it didn't know where to look. As if it was saying, "Hey, kid. Don't do this to me in public."

Too late, yet again. This time too late for the dog. Joel scratched contentedly between its ears. "Good doggy."

The dog tried one more half-hearted growl to scare away his pest. It didn't work. Joel smiled happily in return.

"Oh, nuts," the dog's face said. It flopped to the ground in resignation. Joel climbed on its back and reached around to rub its fat belly.

"That dog is just a pussycat," Mike said as he climbed down from his horse.

He took one step toward the shack. The dog raised its head and bared its teeth. Mike climbed back on his horse.

"Scared of cats?" I asked Mike.

CHAPTER 15

We politely shouted several times for anyone in the shack.

Then we politely—very quietly and very politely—asked Joel to rejoin us.

He did, reluctantly, giving the dog one final pat.

Once Joel was on the horse with me, we gave the dog plenty of room and moved past the shack to follow the mud road. It soon narrowed to a tight trail that led down the ravine. The grass on the path was worn to dirt almost as hard as concrete.

"I saw a county map in the newspaper office," Sarah said to break the silence as we stopped and overlooked the path. "I think this ravine brings us to the downstream side of the Wolf Creek cliffs."

I was much less concerned about geography than I was about a hermit appearing any second with a shotgun and some rope to tie us to trees.

"We should head down there," Mike said. "We'll keep our eyes open for a place where someone might hide cattle. Besides, Ricky hasn't seen the far end of the cliffs yet."

That's all I wanted. Mike for a tour guide through haunted cliffs with a hermit lurking nearby.

Before I could protest, Sarah and Mike spurred their horses onto the path.

We rode single file. A light wind whistled through the trees around us. Within minutes the path leveled and we broke out of the trees into a wide, flat part of the valley.

The sight was so beautiful, for a second I forgot to be scared.

For miles along our left, a huge wall of land loomed abruptly from the broad plains. The plateau of land at the top of that wall was at least five stories above our heads. On that plateau, I realized, Uncle George and Aunt Edith had their ranch.

Cutting through that wall, the gorge of the Wolf Creek cliff spilled down to join the broad plain in front of us. As I looked up the gorge, I saw how the cliff walls twisted and turned along the path of the creek, growing closer together the farther upstream I looked.

From the gorge came a small stream of water that meandered through a grass-filled gully in front of us.

Ahead and to the right, the broad plain of the valley bottom extended for probably half a mile to where the hills began climbing again to the far mountains. Behind us, of course, lay the ravine that led to Quigley's shack.

"You can see how horses can only enter the cliffs from this side," Mike commented.

I was too stunned by the view to say anything.

"I said," he repeated louder, "you can see how horses can only enter the cliffs from this side."

"Sure," I finally replied. He was right. We would have to follow the creek upstream quite a ways to reach the drop-off where we had seen the phantom outlaw the night before.

"So . . ." Mike said.

I finally caught on.

"I don't think that's a good idea, Mike."

He and Sarah were already moving their horses ahead into the canyon formed by the cliffs.

As usual, around Mike I expected the worst. I just didn't expect it to happen so soon. What happened next electrified me as surely as if I had touched Quigley's fence.

We were barely a hundred yards into the canyon before a horse bolted from scrub brush near the next bend.

It wasn't the sudden scrabbling of hooves against rock that electrified me. It was the long blond hair flowing from beneath the cowboy hat of the horse's rider!

"Let's get her!" Mike yelled as he spurred his horse into pursuit. Sarah didn't wait a second before following.

"Are you both lunatics?" I shouted. "That's an outlaw you're chasing!"

All I received for a reply was choking dust from their horses.

"Nuts," I said to Ralphy as Mike and Sarah rounded the bend. "This is not my idea of a peaceful Sunday afternoon."

Ralphy sighed. We both knew one of us would have to go ahead into the canyon to find Mike and Sarah.

"Why don't you stay here," I suggested. "Keep Joel with you and wait half an hour. I hope nothing bad happens up there, but if it does and we don't get back by then, ride back to the ranch."

"How about I wait right at the mouth of the canyon." Ralphy looked into the cliffs towering over us. "It's only a little ways back, and that way nothing can jump on me."

"Good idea," I said. "Just keep hold of Joel's teddy bear so he doesn't move, either."

With that, I did what I didn't feel like doing. I set Joel on Ralphy's horse and urged Sheba farther ahead into the canyon. We didn't gallop. Even after Sarah's riding lessons, I still liked slow-moving horses.

Around the next bend, the cliffs on both sides ran straight for the length of a football field. There was nothing to see except rock and scrub brush and the sheer sides of the cliff walls. I kicked Sheba into a trot and we quickly reached the next bend.

Nothing again. Horse tracks dotted the sand of the creek bed, but there was no other sign of riders. Sheba and I trotted around two more bends—each time my heart pounding louder with apprehension—and still we saw nothing but creek bed, scrub brush, and sheer rock.

The farther ahead we went, the more the gap between the sides of the cliff walls narrowed. *How much longer before it's impossible to continue?* I wondered.

I didn't wonder long. Sheba and I trotted around the fourth bend and nearly collided with Mike and Sarah on their horses. They were alone.

"I can't believe it," Mike said. "I just can't believe it."

"The horse just vanished," Sarah explained. "We were only seconds behind going into this bend, and when we turned the corner, it was gone."

The walls of the canyon were so close they seemed to press in on us. Somehow, I had a prickly feeling on my back. Were we being watched?

"Any tracks?" I asked.

"None straight ahead," Mike said. "And by the time we thought to look, our own horses had trampled the ground here pretty good."

"There's got to be an explanation—" I started to say, but a movement high in the cliffs to my right caught my eye. "Look out!"

Once again, if I had had time to think, I would not have done the right thing. But the danger was so sharp and real that my body moved on instinct.

I reached out, and as hard as I could I slapped Mike's horse, then Sarah's, as a huge boulder left the side of the cliff. Seconds after we galloped ahead, the boulder and a shower of smaller rocks crashed into the spot where we had been standing!

The sliding of pebbles continued for a few more seconds during our stunned silence.

"Whatever you want, Ricky, it's yours," Mike said slowly. "My baseball card collection. My skateboard. My dirt bike."

I didn't reply. I was too busy checking the cliffs for more movement.

"How about a ticket out of here instead," I finally said. "This is a great place to be ambushed. If there is a phantom outlaw, it may be angry."

I didn't have to say it twice.

We turned our horses around and picked our way through the pile of rock that blocked our return to Ralphy and safety.

It wasn't about to work that way. No sooner had we navigated the small landslide when someone stepped in front of us to block our path.

That someone carried a shotgun, and we looked straight into the business end of it.

CHAPTER 16

"Hello, sir," I said as brightly as I could, considering the black holes of his double-barreled shotgun seemed larger than dinner plates. "Have you seen my father nearby? A big fellow. Real big. Maybe six foot six. Unfortunately, as mean as he looks. He was target shooting somewhere around here."

"And boy, is he good," Mike said. "The guy can knock a fly off a baseball bat at a hundred yards."

The man in front of us stared at us blankly. He was as old as Mr. Keyster, the banker, but his skin was less worn by time. His hair was thick and gray, cut ragged around his forehead and ears. One side of his face was deformed, as if he had a baseball stuck inside his cheek. He was dressed in faded cotton work clothes and had a coil of rope around one shoulder.

I had no doubt it was Quigley. Funny, I expected a hermit to have a beard. Which he didn't. But he did dress like a person who lived away from the comforts of civilization.

Then it hit me. Rope! The coil of rope around his shoulder. Maybe he really did tie people to trees. I tried to hide the quiver of fear crashing through my stomach.

He stared at us a few seconds more but didn't say a word.

"It's too bad you haven't seen my large, large father, sir," I said, ignoring my shaking stomach and hoping the bluff would work. "Because I'm sure he's worried about us. Right, Mike?"

"Yup. That's right. Real worried," Mike continued, his

eyes bulging at the sight of the coiled rope. "Well, we'd better be on our way. Maybe we can find his dad soon before he gets too worried. Mean guy, he is. Real mean. And protective."

I shook the reins loose to encourage Sheba to move ahead and around the man with the gun.

He grabbed the reins, stopped Sheba short, and scowled.

"Well," I said slowly. "I guess good old Dad can wait a few more minutes."

The man stared me in the eye. I tried not to flinch.

Still staring, the man turned his face sideways slightly and spit.

It was a huge, drippy spitball, brown and gooey. Then I realized the lump in the side of his face was a tremendous wad of chewing tobacco.

"Son," the old man said in a gentle voice, "that was one of the best stories I've heard in a long time. But I been in this canyon all day, and I ain't seen no pistol-toting giant to match that description."

He paused to spit another huge ball into the sand. "By the way you told it," he added, "a person might think you were scared of an old fellow out hunting foxes."

"Hah, hah," I said. "Imagine that, sir."

"Foxes?" Sarah asked from behind Mike and me.

The old man nodded. Strangely, something about the front of his neck poked at my memory. He must have caught my glance, because he rubbed his neck with his free hand.

"That's right, girl. Foxes. They hang around my house and try to get my chickens."

Mike snorted. "The foxes must be as big as bears not to be scared of that dog."

The man in front of us slowly raised his eyebrows. His silence seemed icy.

Mike turned red. "That is, if you're Quigley—I mean Mr. Spears."

"I'm Quigley Spears all right. And you kids been at my house?" He asked it so quietly that it scared my mouth dry.

"Um, yes, sir," Mike said.

"Some folks around here think trespassing is enough of a crime to hang for."

The rope!

"We weren't trespassing, Mr. Spears," I said. "We were—"

Sarah interrupted me. "It was my idea. We thought we would ask you about the phantom outlaw."

"You kids really were at my house." He caught me glancing at his neck again, and he casually pulled his kerchief above his collar. "I'm not too happy about that. You're lucky that Samson didn't rip you guys apart. I don't like people on my property without my permission."

"But how can we get permission without going on your property to ask you?" Mike said.

"Exactly." The hermit spat again. "Now we'd best be saying good-bye. I've had enough of kids for the day."

Sarah held up her hand. "But, sir, what about the phantom outlaw? Have you seen it? You live close by and—"

"The phantom outlaw," Quigley said thoughtfully and spat once more, splattering sand at his scuffed boots. "Maybe she's there. And maybe she's not. But if I were you, I'd be careful in looking. And you know what else?"

All three of us shook our heads.

"I'd make plenty sure I didn't cut across my property looking for her. Samson can hear a mouse crawling half a mile away, and without that chain around his neck . . ."

Quigley waited and then smiled. "The funny thing is, Samson never gives warning."

He spat one final time, then saluted us good-bye.

He slapped Sheba on the hindquarters, then slapped Mike's horse, then Sarah's. By the time we could look back from our moving horses, he had disappeared among the canyon walls.

CHAPTER  17

"Watch out for that rattlesnake."

"Aaaaaaaaa!" Mike jumped, then realized I was joking. It felt good to see *him* nervous for a change. Me? When I'm mad, I'm too stupid to be nervous.

Halfway up the sun-dried walls of the canyon on Monday morning, we were definitely in rattlesnake country.

"You know, I think this makes us even," he said.

"For what?" I was not in a good mood. Being mad does that to me, too.

"For all the times I have accidentally gotten you into trouble."

"Keep climbing, chowder head."

Sometime the night before, the shakes from nearly being crushed by a landslide had left. The tremors from facing a hermit with a shotgun had quit. Then from sound sleep, I had sat straight up and stared at the dark wall across the room with anger filling my stomach.

If someone deliberately pushed that boulder, I want to know.

I wasn't sure. And I was hoping the boulder had been triggered into action by natural causes. I only knew I had seen a flicker of movement moments before the boulder began crashing down toward us.

Had that movement been a person?

I had grown angrier and angrier and angrier sitting in the dark, thinking about someone trying to scare us—or, worse, kill us.

The only thing that let me sleep again was vowing to

find the answer as soon as possible.

So—after my fight with the stupid cat that wanted to bury itself on my face for the fifth morning in a row—Mike, Sarah, and I went to look for the answer. Our search put Mike and me somewhere on a canyon wall in the middle of the Wolf Creek cliffs.

Mike was a step ahead of me. It was the only way he agreed to the climb. That way, he said, at least he would land on me if he fell backward.

Sarah sat on her horse at the bottom of the canyon, guarding our horses and staring anxiously upward at our progress. Ralphy was back at the ranch, making sure Joel didn't follow us or, worse, catch another barn full of pigeons.

"Can we just assume a gust of wind blew the boulder loose?"

"No chance, Mike. If someone pushed that boulder, I want to know who. And why." I sucked in some air. Climbing was hard work.

Our path was steep, and we had to pick our way around boulders and scrub brush. Occasionally, it was so steep that we had to boost each other over ledges. I was grateful for Sarah's advice to carry a stick and poke ahead into blind spots in case of rattlesnakes. So far, none. Not that I would know what to do—except maybe run—if we saw one.

"If we ever get down," Mike gasped, "I'm going to tie you to Quigley's electric fence and have a marshmallow roast as you sizzle."

"Sissy. If you try that, I'll—"

I grabbed the back of his pants before he could take another step. "Are you nuts?!"

"Shhh!" I said.

Five steps away, coiled and head raised, a huge rattlesnake covered the path. As Mike and I watched in horror, its tail rattled ominously.

"That's enough for me," Mike blurted. "Time to head back." He turned and quickly stepped behind me.

I wanted to run, too. But the thought of someone pushing a boulder down on us made me grit my teeth with anger that drove out fear. I had no idea what to do next. I only knew that I wanted to get past the snake and up the cliff another ten yards to see where the boulder had been loosened.

The slits in the snake's eyes narrowed as I moved closer. A tiny tongue flickered from its triangular head. I poked my stick forward. The snake struck!

The force of its blow nearly knocked the stick from my hand. I was glad Sarah had insisted on giving me a long stick. The snake recoiled itself, but not before I had an idea.

I poked the stick ahead again—this time holding it with both hands—and when the snake struck, the length of its body stretched flat for half a second. I brought the stick down quickly and push-scooped the snake sideways. It hung in the air briefly, then bounced against the side of the cliff and dropped and rolled to a lower ledge. It crawled out of sight.

I had instant regret at trying something so stupid, even if it did work. But having done it, there was no sense in letting Mike see my fear. I put my hands in my pockets to hide their trembling.

"So, uh, you were thinking of threatening me, the rattlesnake kid?" I said as coolly as possible.

"Hah," he said, the blood slowly returning to his face. "You got lucky. Let's get this dumb search over with."

As soon as we reached the spot, I wished we hadn't.

The ground was too hard to show footprints.

But what we saw was worse.

The edge of the depression where the boulder had rested was sharply outlined. At the front and back, however, the edge was chipped, and bits of crushed shale and rock had fallen into the depression.

Mike and I stared.

"Somebody rocked that back and forth," I said. "The depression is too deep for the boulder to have rolled forward by itself. And those loose pieces in there must have chipped from the edges as it was being rocked."

Mike nodded.

Suddenly he put his hand on my shoulder and squeezed hard.

"I can't believe I'm seeing this," he muttered.

Mike bent down and reached for something at his feet. He stood, and between his thumb and forefinger he held a long strand of blond hair that glowed in the sun.

"The phantom outlaw!" Sarah's eyes widened as she saw the long blond hair.

"Is she still your hero?" Mike asked. "She tried to kill us."

"Maybe she just meant to scare us." Sarah snapped her fingers. "And if that's the case, maybe the money is nearby."

We were on our horses, walking through the creek bed. I figured watching for another landslide was more important than speaking, so I was quiet on my horse.

"She's probably got it booby-trapped," Mike said with a sneer. "How can you think she's that great? Now, Robin Hood, there was a fellow. At least he never started landslides on people."

Enough was enough.

"You guys are lunatics," I said. "You're discussing this phantom outlaw as if she really exists. Delilah Abercombe rode into this canyon over fifty years ago. She's not here as a ghost. It's just not possible."

"Fine," Sarah said, "then you explain what we saw yesterday. And why Mike found that clue where the boulder was pushed."

"I can't. I just know there's got to be a logical explanation."

A thought reverberated through my mind. *She's not here as a ghost.*

I pulled on the reins. Sheba rocked to a halt. Sarah and Mike had no choice but to stop. I turned in the saddle to look back at them.

"Try following this logic," I said. "What if the phantom outlaw really is Delilah Abercombe?"

We all thought about it. The wind keened through the canyon walls.

"She died in the storm," Mike said.

"And even if she didn't die, why would she hang around this canyon if she had all the money?" Sarah said.

"And where would she live?" Mike said. "In a tree?"

I shook my head. "Sorry, that was a stupid guess."

"Which puts us back to square one." Mike's face brightened. He pointed behind me. "Hey, look, a coyote!"

I didn't bother turning forward in my saddle. As if I would fall for that one after I fooled him about the rattlesnake during our climb. "Nice try, Mike."

He shrugged.

I turned forward. And nearly fainted. A big bushy-tailed coyote *was* there, stepping out of the bushes about ten feet in front of the horses. Maybe it wanted water so badly it didn't care about our low voices.

It did care about sudden noises, though.

Mike whispered from behind me, "Watch this."

When Mike whistles with his fingers, it sounds like a train screeching its brakes. The high shriek of his whistle nearly broke my eardrums. It also sent the coyote about three feet into the air. It bolted straight ahead.

The coyote's jump shot it almost into Sheba's legs. That sudden movement and the loud noise were all it took. Sheba broke from under me in a sudden rush of hooves and muscle that jerked the reins loose and left me flopping in the saddle.

Not again!

Only this time it was scarier. Instead of grass and wide open hills around Sheba's gallop, there were cliff walls and rocks and scrub brush.

I had to reach the reins!

Slowly I leaned forward, fighting to keep my balance as Sheba pounded down the creek bed.

Two more inches. All I need is two more inches and then I can get my fingertips to the edges of the dangling reins and then—

I looked up in time to see a huge bush blocking sheer rock wall.

What was Sheba doing? We were going to hit the wall head-on. Three more galloping lunges forward and we would both—

Sheba hit the brakes. Because I was leaning so far forward, I couldn't. And didn't.

"Aaaaaaaaaaaaggggghhhhhhh!"

In the split second during my ride through the air, I closed my eyes and squinted my face shut as tight as possible against the pain I knew would come as I crunched into the rock behind the bush.

I felt like part of a cheap comic strip. *Crash, bang, thump,* I rocketed into the bush. My feet flipped over my head and I skidded along my back. Then silence.

I opened my eyes. My head was woozy from the crash. My vision was slightly blurred.

Above me, the thick profusion of branches. Below me, the sand. I gingerly sat up and looked at my legs.

"Aaaaaaaaaaaacccck!"

There was nothing showing below my thighs! Everything else

had mashed right into the rock and disappeared.

I suddenly realized it was true what they said about extreme pain. It mercifully puts you into shock so that you can't feel anything. My legs had crushed into the cliff wall and I couldn't even feel it!

I almost hoped I would bleed to death instead of living without legs. And suddenly I began to cry.

Stupid as it seemed, I could not help myself.

That's how Mike and Sarah found me. Lying on my back, frozen scared beneath the bush, sobbing and sniffling. And I didn't even care that I was crying in front of a girl.

Mike's face was ashen as he crawled under the bush to me.

Sarah was right behind.

"I didn't mean to get Sheba scared," he said. "Are you okay?"

"Sure, Mike," I said, feeling bitter, waiting for the pain to hit. "Don't worry about wrecking the rest of my life."

"It's okay," Sarah said, gently wiping hair away from my forehead. "It'll be okay."

I cried harder. "Right. You try living without legs."

"Without legs?"

"I can't bear to look," I said, and sobbed. "And when the shock ends and the pain finally hits, I don't think I'll be able to take it."

"Oh," she said.

"Oh," Mike said.

They looked at each other.

"Maybe he whacked his head," Mike whispered out of the side of his mouth. "He could be delirious."

"I heard that. How can you make fun of me at a time like this?"

"Ricky," Sarah said, "I don't know how to break this to you, but your legs are just fine."

"What?"

Mike pointed down where my feet should have been. I sat up and looked. And looked again. This time my eyes didn't blur.

Both my legs had shot forward into a round hole in the rock. I had stopped sliding just at the knees.

I still had legs!

And Mike and Sarah were exchanging strange looks.

"Hah, hah, hah," I said. "Nearly had you fooled. Did I do a good job of faking these tears?"

Mike pushed me back down again.

"I said I was joking. You can help me up now."

He kept his hand pressing down on my shoulder and motioned for quiet. "Shhhh!" Mike pointed where my feet were buried.

At first I heard only the buzzing of insects.

Then I heard more.

The mooing of cattle!

I scrambled to a sitting position and pulled my feet back from the cliff. We all peered into the hole. Total blackness.

Mike tossed a pebble. Very faintly, we heard it clatter down the sides of the shaft. Then silence.

"It's a cave down there!" he hissed.

"And that sounds like livestock," I said.

Sarah grinned. "That's one mystery solved."

I grinned back, happy to be the owner of two healthy legs. "Here's a bigger mystery for you."

"What's that?"

"How did all those cattle get through this tiny hole?"

She punched my shoulder.

We left to get Uncle George, a rope, and a flashlight. Somewhere nearby, there had to be a hidden entrance to the cave below.

CHAPTER 18

"Pretend you're a cow," Uncle George said. "Where would you go from here if you were wandering?"

"I still say it's the work of rustlers," Mike said. "Instead of wandering into the cave, the livestock were stolen or led there. Which means you ought to be carrying a rifle or something."

Joel was still at the ranch helping Aunt Edith make lunch. Ralphy, Mike, Sarah, and I were back at the entrance to the Wolf Creek cliffs after racing to the ranch to find Uncle George. He was carrying rope and a flashlight.

"There's one problem with that," he replied, scanning the cliffs as we paused on horseback. "If you pull a gun on someone, you've got to be prepared to use it. Especially if they're armed. No, Mike, if they want cattle bad enough to kill for it, they're welcome to it. Human life is worth much more than livestock."

"I hate it when grown-ups are right," Mike muttered.

"I'm pretending to be a cow, Uncle George," Ralphy said patiently. "What next?"

"Good question. You've been out on this hot, hot range for weeks. What's your biggest concern?"

"Water!" All of us said it at the same time.

"Exactly. There's a little trickle here, but it's barely worth dropping your head for. So you want to find a pool of it. And you wander up into those cliffs, hoping to find it there. Then what?"

The wind ruffled the top of the dry grass. Our silence of

thought was interrupted only by the swishing of the horses' tails.

"You find it or you don't," Uncle George continued. "If you don't find it, you come back. If you do—"

"You stay," I said.

"Unless it's rustlers," Sarah said.

Uncle George ignored her. "Right, Ricky. So the obvious thing is that they did find water. As Ralphy pointed out on our way here, water is usually responsible for the caves created in these limestone formations. Which makes sense, considering where you heard them. Our job is to find an entrance big enough for a cow to walk through."

A thought hit me.

"There's one other thing," I said. "Since the cattle didn't start disappearing until after the storm, maybe we'll find that entrance near a recent landslide or something like that."

Uncle George smacked his forehead. "Of course. Why didn't I think of that before? The storm!"

"Sure, the storm. I knew that, too," Mike said and rolled his eyeballs like we were crazy. When Uncle George pushed ahead without answering, and all of our horses began to follow, Mike finally said, "Okay, Ricky. I'll bite. What does the storm have to do with it?"

"Mr. Keyster, the banker, told us that during a big storm, the creek bed sometimes changes its course completely. Since the cattle didn't find the cave before the storm, the storm must have opened up the entrance somehow. So if we can find a recent landslide—"

"—or something like that, we'll probably find the cave," Mike said. "I knew that. I was just testing you."

"Sure, Mike," I said pleasantly as he watched my face for reaction. Then I looked skyward and opened my eyes in shock.

"A pigeon!"

Mike ducked suddenly and covered the back of his neck with his hat.

"Just testing you," I said as gravely as possible.

We rode in two columns, one on each side of the creek and as close as possible to the walls of the cliffs. The search took us less than fifteen minutes.

Roughly fifty yards from where I thought I had lost my legs, Uncle George pointed to a shed-sized chunk of rock that had been torn away from the cliffs.

"Fresh enough?" he asked. The shredded and crushed bushes

sticking out from the rock still held green leaves. Uncle George dismounted without waiting for our replies.

By the time we had tied our own horses and reached him, he had already found the entrance.

"Walk around back of this mess," he said. "You'll find that the shade is dark because of more than a lack of sunlight."

Mike sprinted ahead of us the five steps it took to get around the rock. "A cave!" he shouted. "I found a cave!"

A door-sized gash into the side of the cliff was shaded almost completely by an overhang of rock. The shade seemed cool. And we could hear the distant lowing of the cattle echoing through the gap.

"They can smell water, you know," Uncle George said. "I'm sure it's the only reason they would even take a step into there."

"But why don't they come out again?" Ralphy said. "Once they've had enough to drink, you'd think they'd get hungry and come back out for some grass."

Uncle George's face became grim. "When you told me about the cave, my first worry was that they had broken their legs on the way down. I hope that's not the reason they're still down there."

He clicked on the flashlight. "Someone should stay out here to watch our horses. Mike?"

"Me? Come on. You can't even see them from here."

"Then I'll show you where they are," Uncle George said gently. He led Mike away from us. That didn't fool me. I guessed Uncle George didn't want us to hear him giving Mike instructions on what to do in case the rest of us got stuck in the cave.

It didn't matter. I wasn't nervous. That's the nice thing about grown-ups. They make you feel secure. My skin would have broken into hives thinking about going into the cave *alone* with Mike and Ralphy.

Besides, how much danger could there be? We could still hear the cattle. And—

"Maybe there are rustlers down there," Sarah said.

She was right. There was a slight chance of some danger.

I didn't have time to think about it. Uncle George returned and stepped in front of Ralphy, Sarah, and me. We followed the beam of his flashlight through the entrance.

The door-sized gap did not widen or narrow as we went deeper, step by slow step, into the cave. The floor of the cave gradually sloped downward. Looking back, I could see the daylight at the entrance grow smaller and smaller.

Even though the restless lowing of the cattle grew louder, we spoke in hushed tones.

"No problem so far," Uncle George whispered. "I wonder what's keeping them down there."

This time Sarah didn't mention rustlers. I was glad for that. In the cramped darkness of the cave tunnel, I was ready to believe rustlers were responsible.

"Oooooooof!"

The beam of the flashlight danced crazily, then snapped off! There was a thud as Uncle George bounced against ground in the darkness, then a clattering of the flashlight, then silence.

"Don't take a step!" Uncle George hissed from somewhere below us. We froze.

I looked back again, comforted by the tiny hole of daylight against the blackness. It was a long climb back out, but the entrance was still there.

"Hang on, kids," Uncle George spoke again. "There's nothing to worry about. I just need to find the flashlight."

A match hissed and flared in the darkness below us. "There it is," he said triumphantly. He scrambled sideways and bent over. The flashlight beam shone again, then pointed to a four-foot ledge a few steps down from where we stood.

"See the drop-off?" Uncle George asked. "If you're smart, you won't take the hard way like I did."

We slowly climbed down.

Uncle George groaned ruefully. "At least that explains why the cattle couldn't get back up again."

The ground leveled, and another dozen steps took us out of the narrow tunnel. A breeze hit my face, as if the opening were part of a large cavern. Uncle George's flashlight confirmed it. High above us, the stone of the cave's roof dimly shone in the beam. Ahead and to the sides, the flashlight beam could not reach any walls.

"Wow!" Ralphy breathed. "This must have taken thousands of years to form. And the water?"

Uncle George threw a pebble ahead in the darkness. *Splash.*

"Sounds deep," he said. "Now, where are the cat—"

He stopped because the beam of the flashlight bounced off tiny white dots waist-high in the blackness.

"Baaaaawwwwwhhh!"

We were being welcomed.

"Bingo," Uncle George whispered in the silence that fell after the bawl of the calf.

"So how do we get them out?" I asked. "Providing they're not hurt from the drop-off."

"If we all pull together, will we be able to lift them one by one over the ledge?" It was Sarah. She didn't sound disappointed that we hadn't found rustlers.

"'Fraid not," Uncle George's voice came at us through the darkness. "I've got the rope to guide them, but we'd need a sling and six strong men to lift."

"There's another way," Ralphy said calmly. "A ramp."

"He's got it," Uncle George agreed. "I'll have to bring some planks from the ranch. At least we know the cattle are here."

"Piling rocks would take forever," I added, "but maybe we can find something else down here to save us the trip."

"I doubt it," Uncle George replied.

"We're down here anyway," Sarah said. "It can't hurt to look."

"It had better not," Uncle George snorted. "I hurt enough from finding the ledge."

So we began to look around.

Two minutes later, against the side of a rock, we found a leather bag stuffed with bills.

"George, you're positive you didn't find any papers with this money?"

"Telling you no three times isn't good enough, Keyster?" Uncle George asked. "We brought the money, and only the money. We didn't bring papers because we couldn't find any."

Uncle George had started off earlier by calling him "Mr. Keyster," then "Fred," and now as he became impatient, just "Keyster." You would think a banker who had been handed more than ten thousand dollars in long-lost cash would be happy instead of so demanding with his questions.

After finding the money bag, we had spent the first part of the afternoon rescuing the cattle with planks hauled from the ranch. Then all of us had gone into town with Uncle George and reached the bank shortly before closing time. Mr. Keyster had smiled his false-teeth smile briefly, then gone back to counting money, until we showed him the old leather bag.

Sarah interrupted the glare Uncle George was giving Mr. Keyster.

"We didn't find a body, either," she said. "So Delilah Abercombe wasn't washed into the tunnel like you said might have happened."

That had been the scary part after finding the money. Wondering if a skeleton was nearby.

"A criminal's corpse is the least of anybody's concerns. I merely wanted to know if you had stumbled across any papers."

"I thought you said they were worthless property deeds," I told Mr. Keyster.

"Quite worthless. Understand? Quite worthless. But finding them now would help on our paperwork and insurance and things like that. Nothing for you kids to bother your heads about."

I gritted my teeth. Grown-ups treat you three ways. One way is buddy-buddy, which only makes you lose respect because you instinctively know there should be a difference between you and them. Another way—like Keyster's—is to treat you like a helpless baby. Or the best way, when they give you respect, the way where you both feel equal but still different because of age and experience.

I was losing respect fast for Mr. Keyster. He had his money, but he didn't seem grateful.

Mike proved how little gratitude Mr. Keyster had. "How about the reward, Mr. Keyster? The paper said there was a thousand dollars for solving the bank robbery."

"Finding the money doesn't solve it," Mr. Keyster snapped.

"Keyster, you said she was dead and the papers were worthless." Uncle George's eyes blazed. "What else is there to solve? These kids deserve something for returning the money."

"The reward expired twenty years ago, George. If they want to open savings accounts here, I'll make sure I waive all service charges. Now, if that's all for today, I have a bank to tend to."

No service charges. And we could come back each summer to deposit more money. Lucky us.

CHAPTER  19

Tuesday morning the four of us—Mike, Sarah, Ralphy, and I—stood in front of the entrance to the cave. After rescuing the cattle the day before, we had barricaded it by driving in fence posts on each side and hammering two-by-four pieces of lumber across to keep cattle out.

"Ricky Kidd, I can't believe *you* insisted on this," Sarah said as we stared past the barricade at the dark, dark opening into the cliff wall. "Mike, maybe. Me, for sure. But you hate this kind of thing."

"That banker was too strange yesterday," I said. "It drives me nuts not knowing why. You'd think he might be more excited about getting his money back."

"The guy owes us a reward," Mike grumbled. "As soon as we found that money, I started dreaming about a hot new skateboard."

"Or some new programs for my iMac," Ralphy added wistfully.

"He did weasel out of the reward part," I agreed. "But think. There's got to be a reason the *original* property deeds are so important to Mr. Keyster."

Ralphy mopped his forehead against the morning heat. "Maybe the location of the deeded property is important. Like I said before, we could always do a title search instead of going back into the cave."

Leave it up to Ralphy to know that the land titles division at the county courthouse kept a public record of all real estate transactions.

"Right," I said. "We can wait a couple of days and sort through tons of records and pay a fee for the search. That way, instead of a reward, finding the bank money will actually cost us. That sounds like a smart way of doing things."

"What could go wrong here, Ralphy?" Mike asked. "We've got flashlights. The cattle aren't down there anymore. And it's only a three-minute run back to the entrance. It would be terrible if *you* couldn't go some place that a girl didn't mind going."

"Nuts," Ralphy said.

He squeezed through the barricade after us and followed as we descended the narrow tunnel.

Once again a cool breeze hit our faces as we stepped from the tunnel into the cavern.

"Let's assume Delilah Abercombe did bring both the money and the deeds down here," I said, my voice echoing throughout the darkness. "Then the deeds are probably close by."

Sarah remained silent. But in the daylight, before entering the cave again, I had seen the intensity in her eyes and clenched jaw. I knew she was as excited about this as we were.

We scattered throughout the cavern, which was about the size of a baseball infield. The pool in the center was only ten or twelve feet wide. Our flashlight beams flickered in every direction.

I didn't think it would be difficult to find the papers. The day before, because of the cattle and the excitement of finding the money, we hadn't done much more looking. Now we were determined to uncover Keyster's secret.

I heard a slight scuffle behind me where the tunnel led into the cavern. I shone my light but saw nothing. Imagination, I was sure. I'm always jumpy in the dark.

"Here it is!" Mike shouted. "The other half of the saddlebag!"

He squeezed his flashlight between his knees to shine its beam at the rock where we had found the money the day before, scrabbled in the dirt with his free hands, and pulled at a corner piece of leather.

Two tugs and it was free.

"Ricky, check this out!"

Mike shone the flashlight into the bag and pulled out some certificates. I ran over and handed my own flashlight to him so he could shine both on the deeds.

I squinted to look carefully.

"I can't figure this out," I said. "There doesn't seem to be any-thing unusual about this. Why would Keyster want them back?"

I dug deeper into the pouch to the musty smell of damp leather.

"Hang on, guys," I grumbled. Sarah and Ralphy had almost toppled over Mike's shoulder trying to see inside.

"Here's another deed. This one with a scribbled piece of paper attached. Let's see." I quickly scanned it. "Dated December 1, 1944. *I, Sam Abercombe, being of sound mind and body, declare the intent to sell my land in Wolf Creek County to Reginald Keyster for prevailing market prices.*"

"Nothing strange there," Mike said over my shoulder. "Maybe that last piece of paper explains more."

"It looks like—" I carefully unfolded the faded paper— "a letter. But I can barely see the writing. Move the light clos—"

"Did you hear something?" Ralphy's voice quavered.

There was nothing but silence and darkness outside the circle of light cast by our flashlights.

Mike snorted. "Maybe it's Delilah Abercombe's ghost come back to stop us from disturbing her treasure."

"That's not funny, Mike," Ralphy said. "Ghosts make me afraid. Afraid makes me throw up. And you know I hate throwing up."

Mike shone the flashlight up his own nose and widened his eyes gruesomely.

I sighed.

"Knock it off. We need the light on this paper, Mike."

He directed the beam onto the letter.

The ink was faint, so I held the letter six inches from my nose to read.

"This letter is dated January 21, 1945!" I said. "From Belgium!"

They crowded closer. I read out loud slowly and carefully.

Dear Delilah,

What do you write to someone you may never see again, except to say I love you. Three simple words, my little one. I love you.

I pray they will be enough, but as a father, there was so much more I wanted to do for you. It's hard to let go. After your mother died, I was the one who bandaged your knees, helped you through fevers, and yes, even fixed your dolls. I want desperately to be there now as you grow into womanhood.

But I don't think this war will let me.

We are at the front of the war zone, and the fighting grows fiercer every day. I am sending this letter to a friend in Paris. It contains all the money I have managed to save. He will deliver it to you as soon as the war ends, which I pray is soon.

There are two things I want you to know.

First, my fears for your future are eased when I think of how much the land you inherit will be worth. An oil company surveyed it just before the war began and their geologists told me there is a good possibility they can strike a gusher. You were too young to understand at the time; then the war stopped their exploration, so this, I'm sure, will be news to you. What it means is that should I die here in Europe, do not sell the land. I repeat. No matter how short of money you become, do not sell the land. When the war ends, and companies turn their attention to making money again, you will find the oil rights to be worth a fortune.

The second thing is this. I understand why you screamed at me with rage as I left you at the train station on my last day in Montana. A father should not have to leave someone he loves, but I could not let this country fight without me. The things you shouted at me in your frustration are things I know you didn't mean. Delilah, I'm afraid that if I don't return, you will be haunted by those last words to me. But don't let them haunt you. A few quick words of anger cannot fool me into forgetting a lifetime of love. I remember always the many good things we did together. That is the way I think of us. Doing many good things together. If you remember me that way, too, then I did manage to do part of my job as a father. Please forgive me for not doing more.

Love,
Sam Abercombe

The last thing I expected in the silence that followed was a muffled sobbing from behind Mike.

It was Sarah.

Mike and Ralphy and I stared awkwardly at each other.

"Sarah . . ." I started.

"Leave me alone," she said. She walked into the darkness.

I made a move to follow. Mike grabbed my arm.

"Don't," he whispered. "Remember her own father."

I nodded, then slowly folded the letter and placed it into my back pocket. The three of us sat mutely, not knowing what to do or say.

How could Sam's letter make sense? I wondered. *The paper attached to the property deed had already sold the land to Mr. Keyster. And it was dated December 1944. Yet barely a month later, he writes to Delilah and tells her not to sell under any circumstances.*

But I couldn't ask aloud in the silence left after Sarah's tears. We didn't even risk looking at more of the papers, because the crinkling sounded like thunder. It felt like five minutes passed as Sarah's choked sobs became quieter and quieter.

We heard a faint scraping.

Then Sarah screamed a brief high scream, more terrifying because of its shortness and intensity.

Mike, Ralphy, and I stood in horror. Before we could move farther, Sarah was pushed into the beams of our flashlights by a man carrying a huge hunting knife.

"Mr. Keyster!" Mike hissed in instant recognition.

"Knock off the dramatics, kid. Just hand me the pouch."

CHAPTER  20

Mike hesitated. The banker placed his knife point lightly on the skin under Sarah's chin. Mike gave him the pouch immediately.

"The letter that Ricky just read out loud, too."

"Letter?" Mike asked.

Keyster sighed and lightly jabbed the knife. A tiny pin-prick of blood formed a dark red ball on her neck. Tears and dirt streaked Sarah's face, but she set her jaw and remained silent.

"I've got the letter," I said very quickly.

As I reached behind me, I remembered the last thing I had done before going to sleep the night before. I had started a letter home to tell Mom and Dad about discovering the bank money. Except I hadn't finished, and when I woke, I had stuffed it in my pocket to work on later.

Don't mix up the letters, Ricky Kidd, I told myself. *What if he hurts Sarah?*

Then I had another thought, a hunch. I made a split-second decision, not knowing why, and not knowing why it might be important. And it was a gamble. I deliberately pulled the wrong letter from my pocket and, stretching my hand across the flickering lights, gave it to the banker.

"Thank you," he sneered.

I knew I had to distract him before he could unfold it.

"This is crazy, sir," I said. "Why do you need these old papers so badly?"

"Funny you should ask." But he didn't smile. "Because I

think you can figure it out from the letter you just read so touchingly to your friends."

Click. A major league light bulb flashed in my head.

"Those abandoned oil wells outside of Wolf Creek," I said. "That was Sam Abercombe's land!"

"Brilliant, Sherlock," he said with no expression. "Continue."

"The war," I said, remembering the old photograph filled with young soldiers that I had seen in the bank. "Coming from the same area, you and Sam Abercombe were in the same unit together in Europe. You must have found out about the oil exploration from him."

Mr. Keyster nodded coldly. "He confided in me. Those things happen when men are afraid of dying." The banker's bushy gray eyebrows threw sinister shadows across his forehead.

"Sam died in the war," I continued, my theory becoming more certain in my head as I spoke. "And you didn't. So when you got back here, you took the land from his daughter, Delilah."

"Took?" Mr. Keyster said distastefully. "In 1945, at the end of the war, she was fourteen years old and an orphan. I bought it from her so she would have enough money to live on. I gave her fair market value."

"Fair market value before she knew about the oil money, or after?" I said.

"That's enough talk for today, kid."

Mike spoke out. "In other words, she didn't know about the oil."

Silence.

The banker started unfolding the letter.

"But if you bought it, why were these old deeds so important?" I asked quickly.

Mr. Keyster sighed, refolded the letter without looking at it, and placed it in his vest pocket.

"Because of this letter. Sam's war buddy in Paris died, too. With the confusion in Europe after the war, it took until 1950—a year after the land started producing oil—for the letter to finally get to Delilah. When she read it, she marched into the bank and accused me of fraud. I told her that was ridiculous, that her father had signed a declaration of intention to sell while he was in Europe. She demanded to see it. I refused."

Sarah ignored the knife against her throat and spoke contemptuously. "You refused because you knew the declaration was phony. If

she saw the handwriting, she could prove it wasn't her father's sig-
nature."

Now the dates of the letters made sense. "And you didn't know
about Sam's letter to Delilah when you faked the declaration," I said,
"but by the time the land started producing oil, it didn't matter. As
long as Delilah couldn't prove anything, it would stay yours."

"You kids are much too clever for your own good," Keyster said
in a chilling tone. "Delilah came to the same conclusion. She was a
hothead, and she robbed the bank for my property deeds, intending to
get handwriting experts to prove the letter of sale was fake. I delayed
her at the bank as long as I could, hoping the sheriff would arrive. I
also stuffed money into her bag to make her look like a common thief
when they caught her."

He suddenly pushed Sarah forward. She stumbled into all three of
us. "Sorry, kid," he said, "but I was getting tired of you."

Keyster then continued. "She probably dumped the saddlebags in
this hiding spot and went back out again to escape the posse while
the storm was giving such good cover," he said calmly. "When Delilah
died in the storm, the secret died with her. Until now."

Until now.

I wasn't happy with the tone of his voice and the look in his eyes
as he said that.

"It's going to have to remain a secret awhile longer. Right, kids?"

"Sure. We won't tell," Mike promised.

Keyster laughed, and crazed echoes bounced off the cavern walls.

"No," he said when he got his breath back. "I don't think that's a
workable solution."

He looked at us and rubbed his chin.

"I could kill all of you," he said thoughtfully. "But I hate such
drastic measures.

"You'll just have to stay in the cave until I get my financial affairs
straight and leave the country."

"That's just a couple of hours?" Ralphy asked hopefully.

"More like days," Keyster said, his tone growing chillier. "Fortunately, men of my intelligence prepare for the worst. Which is what I
did by following you to this cave. You'll stay here. I guarantee it."

"We promise," Mike said solemnly.

"Good for you," the banker said. "And to help you keep that promise, I brought some dynamite to seal the cave entrance."

"Dynamite!" I nearly shouted. "We'll never get out!"

"Kid," he replied coldly, "I don't murder. There's water down here to drink. This is the first place they'll look when they notice you missing, and from above they'll think it was only an unlucky cave-in. It'll take them a couple of days to dig you out. By that time I'll be long gone."

Before we could reply, he struck a match and dropped it into the saddlebag. The papers inside flared, and as they burned, he pulled my letter home from his pocket and dropped it into the flames.

"There," he said proudly. "No proof. Even if they believe your story, they won't have evidence enough to provide them a reason to try tracking me down."

He paused and waved his arms. "Back away from that tunnel. When the dynamite blows, it will send a blast of hot air straight down." He smirked. "We don't want you getting hurt."

If there was any chance at all of getting the old banker, it was while he was waving, while his hands were out from his sides, while that dangerous hunting knife was not prepared to strike.

Only sheer desperation would have made me ignore the odds of managing to knock him down and take the knife before he could react. And sheer desperation was there.

So I dived.

Even as I was ramming his stomach, I knew it was too late. He was quicker and stronger than I thought for such an old man. I flailed at his arms but managed only to graze his sleeves. The knife flashed in the light of the dying flames, and something much too hard struck the side of my head.

CHAPTER 21

What brought me out of my blackness was the tremendous *boom* of detonating dynamite and the *whoosh* of hot air blowing into the cavern.

I sat up quickly and bumped into softness and fragrant hair.

"Ricky," Sarah said, "you're alive."

My skull told me that sitting up quickly had been dumb. Movement made my head feel like it was shaking into a million pieces. Above and behind my ear a massive bump throbbed in wallops.

So Keyster had hammered me with the handle of the knife, not the blade.

In the darkness, Sarah repeated herself. "Ricky, you're alive."

"I don't think so," I said.

Ralphy followed the beam of his flashlight to where Sarah was leaning over me.

"We're in trouble," he said flatly.

That terrified me the most, his calmness. Ralphy is never calm.

"Oh?"

"Keyster set up the blast near the top of the tunnel," Ralphy continued in the same flat voice. "That way, he told us, the rescuers' digging would be easy."

"Wonderful," I said.

"He didn't count on the fracturing effect of the blast."

"What do you mean by that, Ralphy?" Sarah asked.

Mike spoke from the darkness behind him. "He means the entire tunnel collapsed. Rescuers can dig a ton a day until next summer and still not reach us here."

Don't let anyone ever tell you that God won't be there when you need Him.

We shut all our flashlights off except one to conserve the batteries. Why, I don't know. We had been sealed in so completely, it didn't matter if we had thirty seconds' or thirty days' more battery power.

Then we did the only thing we could do besides wait. We prayed.

When I say we felt His presence, I'm not going to say God was there asking, "Hey, kids, how are you doing?" No, God was there the best way He's always there for us. Giving peace.

There was no way out; we were going to die. But with God there, somehow we knew that our hope was not limited to something as short as our lives here on earth. I mean, you might live to be eighty years old, and that's still not much compared to eternity. Sitting there huddled around one flashlight beam, we were cloaked with a calm, certain knowledge there was nothing to be afraid of. Not with God on our side.

Sarah broke the hushed silence. "Thanks for reading that letter, Ricky."

I snorted. "Reading it forced Keyster to leave us here."

"I know," she said. "But it took a big load off my shoulders. You know that my dad . . . that he . . . that last fall he . . ."

"Yes," I said as gently as I could. He had died the fall before. I remembered her sobbing in the darkness. I remembered Mike telling me that she never spoke about it.

"It was a tractor, you know," she said slowly. "Some brush got caught in the front axle while he was clearing land. He left the tractor running and went forward and leaned underneath to pull the brush free. The tractor slipped out of neutral, rolled forward, and caught him with the rear tires."

Sarah's breath grew uneven.

Mike started. "Sarah, you don't need to—"

"I need to finish, Mike. He was like that for half a day, with the tractor on top of him. Half a day. And all I can think of was how I had screamed at him just before he left to clear the land. You see, he didn't want me going into town that night to see a movie with my friends. So I had a temper tantrum and screamed at him."

We said nothing.

"Don't you get it?" she said. "The last things he ever heard from me were the most terrible words I could think to say. And he had a half day of dying to think about it."

The letter. Delilah Abercombe shouting with anger at Sam as he left her alone in Montana.

"And now you believe that your dad knew better?" I quietly asked. "That he wouldn't let a few words fool him into forgetting a lifetime of love."

Sarah's tears quietly pattered the ground.

"He bled some during that half day," she said with a distant voice. "And from where he was lying, he reached above him to the side of the tractor tire. With his finger, he used his blood to write the word *love* on the tire."

What she was saying was so important to her that I didn't want to breathe.

"Because I had yelled at him so mean, I never believed he meant that word for me. Only for my mother. But after hearing Sam's letter, it's like I know he did love me. That he meant his last word for both of us."

Her tears broke into sobs again, like water breaking a dam. Except they were happy sobs.

Strange, I thought, Sarah finding her father's love again, only to have what little time was ahead in the cave to enjoy it.

Mike put his arms around her and she cried into his shoulder.

Half an hour later, the first flashlight went out.

I clicked mine on, and Sarah—once again—broke the silence that had lasted the entire half hour.

"Throw another log on the fire, guys." She giggled.

"A big log," Mike said sourly. "This isn't a movie, you know. Nobody's going to rescue us at the last minute."

That shut us up for a while longer.

"Mike," I said, "if this is it for us, I want to confess something."

"Like what?" he demanded suspiciously.

"Remember the day someone tied your shoes together after you fell asleep in Mr. Evans' math class?"

"You mean the day he woke me up by asking me to come to the board to answer a question? The day I fell across two aisles and broke one desk and shattered Evelyn Beingessner's glasses? The day I had to sit in the principal's office and nobody would ever tell me who tied them together?"

"That day," I said.

"No, I don't remember a bit of it," he said grumpily.

"Well, I want to confess," I said and paused. "Ralphy did it."

Ralphy yelped in rage.

"That's okay, Ralphy," Mike said. "Your squealing pal over there is the one who snuck into your house and packed purple Kool-Aid crystals into your showerhead the morning you had to give a speech in front of the whole school. Remember? You looked like a Martian for two days."

I yelped in rage at Mike.

"Hey," Ralphy said to me. "Relax. Mike's the one who keeps putting catnip into your pillow at the ranch. He's the one who keeps letting that ugly farm cat into your room in the morning. We kill ourselves laughing every time you wake up with it on your face."

Mike added with a chortle, "And don't forget the other ugly farm cat that keeps trying to get at the catnip in Sarah's pillow."

Sarah and I shot startled glances at each other. "I hate cats," she said.

The humor of it hit me so hard that I rolled over laughing and banged my sore head on Ralphy's knee. Between cries of pain and howls of laughter, they had no idea what noise I was making. Which set all of them into roaring laughter.

The second flashlight went out.

And Joel dropped his teddy bear onto my lap.

CHAPTER 22

"Hey, everybody," Joel said to us in the darkness. "Look at this cool stone I found."

As if his playing in the dirt was the most important thing to think about. "Joel," I groaned. "Why you?"

"Followed you from ranch," he said proudly.

I stood and kicked with anger in the darkness, half hoping to break my toes against a rock. *Why does Joel have to be in this tomb with us?*

Tears of rage and frustration streamed from my eyes. I could not help myself. We, at least, had been partially responsible for putting ourselves into this situation. Joel had been completely innocent. Yet he was as doomed as we were.

Mike clicked on the third flashlight to see where I was. The light hit my eyes, and I put up my hands to protect myself. "Knock it off, Mike," I snarled. "And leave me alone."

I wandered blindly around the edges of the cavern, ignoring them huddled around the small ray of light.

My crying had stopped but had left wetness against my face. As I walked near the edge of the pool, a small breeze cooled the drying tears.

A small breeze cooled the drying tears!

Of course! How had we found the cave in the first place?

"Guys," I shouted. "Come here. And bring the flashlight."

Suddenly there was hope, and my throat tightened in fear that it might be false hope.

"Ralphy," I said when they stood beside me. "Where do

you suppose the water comes from to fill this pool?"

"Through the limestone, of course."

"Remember where my feet slid and we first heard the cattle?"

"Exactly." He smacked his fist into an open palm. "Why didn't I think of that? Overflow from the creek would go down the shaft and fill this pool. Because of the dark and the cool down here, the water would evaporate very slowly and refill during the next storm up top."

"My question is this," I said. "Do you think that shaft is the same width all the way up?"

Our excited breathing filled the silence as he thought. "No reason why not," he finally said. "Limestone dissolves at an even rate."

"Great," Mike exclaimed. "We can just climb out!"

"Maybe," I said. "Maybe not. Hand me the flashlight."

I played the beam across the ceiling of the cavern. We spotted the opening of the shaft.

It angled in diagonally where the ceiling and the wall of the cavern met. A smooth wide groove in the rock of the wall showed where the water had flowed each time into the pool below.

"Hah, hah," Mike laughed. "Our escape route."

"Something has escaped you, pal," Ralphy said soberly. "The opening of the shaft is at least twenty-five feet above our heads. How do you propose we get there?"

To have our hopes slammed shut like that hurt much worse than first believing we were sealed in forever. All of us stared mutely at the shaft impossibly high above our heads.

"Where's Joel?" I asked. In the rush of excitement, they had left Joel in the darkness on the other side of the cave.

A small hand pressed into mine. I nearly jumped out of my skin.

"Don't worry, guys, I found him." Then an idea slowly crept into my mind. I tried rejecting it at first. But it wouldn't leave. I didn't want to talk about it, but I had no choice.

I spoke slowly, wishing my argument could be wrong. "Trying nothing means we all die in here. So we have nothing to lose by sending someone up the shaft."

"We can't reach it," Mike said. "You know that."

"Maybe," I replied. "But if we use the wall for support, I can stand on Mike's shoulders, and Ralphy on my shoulders, and Sarah on Ralphy's shoulders, and Joel on top of Sarah. I think Joel could reach it then. If he gets stuck, though . . ."

I didn't want to voice my fear. To be trapped in the shaft would be much worse than being trapped in this cavern with the rest of us, with water to drink and friends to pray with.

"I know what you're thinking," Sarah said quietly. "Joel isn't old enough to recognize the risk or old enough to make the choice himself."

Which meant I had to decide for all of us. My mind flashed back to my last decision about Joel. Him sitting under the tree with his teddy bear, sad at spending the summer alone. It squeezed my heart. Could I send him up the shaft to possibly a horrible fate alone? Or would I spare him the risk and condemn him to die with all of us down here?

Another thought hit me. If he made it through, what then? Could the rest of us, even if someone lowered a rope? Was the shaft wide enough for twelve-year-olds?

Too many *if*s.

And suddenly only one answer.

"We've got to send him," I said. "Not sending him would be giving up. And Joel's a fighter."

As if in answer, Joel patted my hand.

CHAPTER  23

You would think that with three others lying beside you, a dropping bucket attached to a rope might hit one of *them* in the head. Or that if it did hit your head, it would at least miss the bump behind your ear that was still throbbing like crazy.

No.

We had fallen asleep beneath the shaft, exhausted by worry. Would Joel make it? Would it be dark by the time he got to the top? Would he be able to get back to the ranch? And worst of all, how would the rest of us get out?

Naturally, the bucket landed on my head. Naturally, it landed squarely on the bump behind my ear.

So I shouted with joy.

I started dancing in the darkness. Until Mike clicked our final flashlight on and caught me in the middle of a hop.

"The bucket!" I said. "Joel made it to the ranch!"

Mike hugged me. I hugged Ralphy. All three of us hugged Sarah. She said, "Um, guys, it's hard to breathe. Why not check the bucket."

"Right," Mike said, clearing his throat. "Good idea."

A note attached to the handle of the bucket read, "Tug twice when you get this."

I tugged twice. Someone at the top tugged back!

But can we squeeze through the shaft? Or is it too narrow?

As if reading my mind, the note continued. "Instructions per person. One, peel down to your underwear. Two, grease yourself thoroughly. Three, grease yourself again. Four, loop the rope around your hands. Five, tug four quick tugs to signal 'ready.' Six, let us pull you up."

I laughed. "We have a chance! This bucket is filled with car grease."

"Who goes first?" Mike asked.

I stopped laughing. *Joel made it. But he's half our size. Is the shaft wide enough all the way to the top? If the first person makes it, we all can. If the first person doesn't...*

"Pick straws?" Ralphy suggested.

"Sure," I said. "Just give me a second to go up there and grab a couple. We seem to be all out down here."

Silence.

"Not a good joke, huh?" I continued. "Look, I'll go first. It was my idea to find the letter. But you have to promise one thing. Shut the flashlight off as I grease myself. I'm kinda shy about my underwear."

It hurt to be pulled straight up by a rope around my wrists. My arms felt as if they were being yanked out of my shoulder sockets. And I didn't mind for a second.

The first twenty-five feet through the air were easy, despite that pain. It was the shaft that became terrible.

I tried not to think of the consequences of getting stuck as I first bumped into the rock of the shaft. The rope kept its steady pressure, and slowly I slid upward. My shoulders and waist banged into the side of the shaft.

Because my hands were above me, I was as streamlined as possible. The grease made the sliding much easier. I was grateful that centuries of water had smoothed the rock.

From thump to thump I slowly moved upwards. The shaft was inclined at an angle barely possible for anyone to crawl without help. How Joel had done it was beyond me, but I knew I would be thanking him for quite some time.

The yanking pain in my shoulders started to become unbearable, but I had no choice. Even with choice, I would have gladly taken the excruciating tearing, because it meant I was being pulled upward.

Suddenly the sure upward progress stopped. I was caught between two protrusions of the shaft!

Don't panic, I told myself. *Don't panic.*

I wiggled once, dangling helpless from the rope that held my wrists. The rough hemp cut sharply into the skin below my hands.

Ignore the pain, I told myself. *Wiggle again.*

Once, twice more. On the third wiggle I broke free.

For an eternity more, the upward pressure tore at my shoulders. Then, just as I was sure my arms were going to rip from my body, I hit light!

Suddenly I was shivering and crying in the moonlight that bathed the Wolf Creek cliffs.

Uncle George caught me as I fell.

Aunt Edith wrapped a blanket around me.

Joel giggled at the grease on my face.

And one of the three strong men who had been pulling on the rope pointed at my bare leg and foot.

"Son, what's that?"

Joel smiled and jumped forward. He recognized my cargo.

"A teddy bear, sir."

"I'm sorry I asked," he said.

Joel untied the shoelace around my ankle, the shoelace attached to the arm of his teddy bear.

It was good to be alive.

CHAPTER 24

"Ricky, if what you say about Keyster is true, it can wait until morning," Uncle George said. "Aunt Edith and I are more worried about getting some food and a good night's sleep into you kids."

Ralphy, Mike, and Sarah were all up safely. Sarah had gone last, after making us promise to close our eyes when she reached the surface. Their greased heads stuck out of their blankets.

"He's trying to leave town," Mike protested.

Aunt Edith interrupted quietly. "This whole story is hard enough to believe already. It won't help if you burst into town at midnight looking the way you are now."

The three neighbor men watched us quietly with doubting expressions. I guess coming up with a teddy bear tied to your foot is one way of ruining your credibility.

"Does anybody know about this rescue attempt?" I asked.

"No one beyond us here."

"I'll bet," I said, examining the looks of disbelief on even Uncle George and Aunt Edith's face, "that none of you are in a real hurry to announce this whole thing to Mr. Keyster anyway." That, at least, brought grins. "I am pretty hungry," I said. "And a shower would feel great." It would be more satisfying to face Mr. Keyster in the morning when he least expected us.

"Mr. Keyster, I hate to be bothering you like this," the sheriff said. "But these youngsters insist on bringing in a tall tale."

Mike, Ralphy, Sarah, and I stood behind the wide body of the sheriff. He had taken his hat off in respect.

Midmorning sun poured in through the front window of the bank and bounced off the spotless floors. Uncle George and Aunt Edith were at the *Wolf Creek Gazette*, trying to confirm some of the particulars of our story. Joel was outside on the sidewalk. I had tied his teddy bear to the bumper of the parked truck to keep him close by.

"Jim, you know I love entertainment." Mr. Keyster smiled at the sheriff. Not even a flicker on his face or a twitch of his bushy eyebrows to show surprise. "What have these youngsters got for us this morning?"

"What have we got?!" Mike shouted. "Yesterday you tried killing us!"

The banker continued his polite smile. "Jim, is this a joke?"

The sheriff shuffled awkwardly. "That's what I think. But these kids insist that you followed them to the cave where they found the money and that you dynamited them in there."

Finally the banker's face showed surprise. "That's an amazing tale, all right," he said. "Why would I do that?"

"Well," the sheriff began uncertainly, "they did have to be rescued from a cave-in last night."

"A cave-in! I'm so glad they're okay!"

I had to hold Mike back from attacking the banker. "You jumped Sarah and put a hunting knife to her throat." Mike's face turned purple with frustration.

To prove it, Sarah lifted her head. A small bruise circled the crust of blood where the knife had broken skin.

Something about her neck bothered me, set off a nagging in the back of my mind. I ignored it, thinking about the surprise I had for the banker, a surprise I hadn't shown the sheriff.

"Jim, I'm beginning to lose patience. A fantasy game of hide-and-seek is one thing. But to accuse me of that . . ."

"Mr. Keyster, they told me a long story about property deeds and the war and such stuff," the sheriff said, tiredly running his fingers through his hair. "It nearly made sense. I'm just hoping you can straighten it out so we can send them on their way again. With a stern warning, of course."

"Well, sheriff, I am a busy man. I'll give you five minutes. Then I want you to do something more than a stern warning. This is beyond a joke." Keyster's face darkened.

Finally I spoke. "I can settle all of this right now."

I looked for the old war photograph. In its place was a scenic photograph of the mountains.

"The photograph you had there two days ago—" I pointed.

Keyster smiled coldly. "It fell off the wall yesterday when the cleaner was dusting it. Shattered."

I pretended I was beaten.

Then I straightened. "We've already explained everything to the sheriff," I said. "Including how you burned the property deeds and the letter from Sam Abercombe."

I wanted badly to see Keyster's smug smile crack.

"But what you don't know," I continued, "is that I switched letters on you. The letter you burned was one I had been writing home to my parents."

It worked. Keyster's face faltered, but only briefly.

"Yes, sheriff," I said triumphantly. "The letter is right here!"

"That's right. We sure fooled you," Mike crowed. Which killed me. Because in the excitement, I hadn't even told him.

I reached into my back pocket.

Nothing.

How could I be so stupid?

The jeans I had worn yesterday were still in the cave. Between eating, sleeping, and getting ready to put Keyster in jail, I had completely forgotten that tiny but important detail. Greasing down had meant leaving my clothes behind in the cave. *Stupid, stupid, stupid.*

I pulled my empty hands from behind my back. "I did have it, sir," I said to the sheriff. "Only it's still in the cave."

Mike shook his head sadly.

"Funny," Mr. Keyster said. "Still in the cave. And you have a way of getting it?"

Fuming, I shook my head.

"Sheriff, I think that's a good indication that they're only trying to pull a stunt. The only reason I can see for this is that they're mad about the expired reward for the bank robbery."

Mr. Keyster stopped, then bent at the knees to look at us at eye level. I noticed one of his sleeve cuffs flapping loose.

"Children," he said in a greasy voice, "I understand your anger. But it's not my fault there's no reward money. Because of all of this, I'm going to forgive all of you."

He looked at the sheriff again. "Jim, just let them be. I hold no grudges."

Mr. Keyster led us to the door and smiled sweetly at our departure. We were too numb to say anything.

On the sidewalk, the sheriff turned to speak to us. Joel, patiently waiting in front of the truck for his teddy bear to be released, ignored us and concentrated on an object in his hands.

"Whatever game you kids are playing has gone too far," the sheriff said. "You should just be grateful you got out of the cave alive. And that Mr. Keyster won't press charges. We'll have no more of—"

Joel. Sweet Joel.

"Sheriff," I interrupted. "Give us one more shot. Please."

Joel rolled the object between his hands, squinting at it in the sunlight.

"Son," the sheriff rumbled a deep warning. "I just told you—"

"I know, sir. But I forgot to mention that just before Mr. Keyster left to dynamite the entrance, I tried tackling him. It didn't work. All I managed to do was slide my hand across one of his arms. There's still a bump on my head where he hit me with the handle of the knife."

"That's it, son. You just pushed me too hard."

I simply grinned at the sheriff's anger.

What had Joel said in the cave? *Look at this cool stone I found.*

"Sir, would you mind taking a close look at the pebble my brother picked up from the floor of the cave?"

Joel scowled as the sheriff gently pried it from his tiny hands.

"This is a cuff link, son."

"Exactly. A garnet cuff link." *The cuff links Mr. Keyster had been so proud of during our first visit.* "Is there any chance you can go back in there and apologize for us to Mr. Keyster? And while you're there, maybe check his sleeves? Without mentioning what my brother found?"

The sheriff frowned at me thoughtfully, then spun on his heel and walked back into the bank.

When he returned, his eyes were puzzled. "The cuff link matches, son. But it's not enough to prove you right and him wrong."

I had visions of dropping a grappling hook into the cave and trying to recover my blue jeans. "It might take days to get the letter, if at all," I said. "And by then, Mr. Keyster will be gone."

"If he's guilty," the sheriff corrected me.

"Is there anything else that would help our case?" Sarah said.

The sheriff tossed the cuff link into the air and grabbed it again with a big palm. "With the letter gone and the deeds burned, there's only one person to verify this."

"Delilah Abercombe," Sarah said, tilting her head with a faraway look in her eyes. The sun's shadow beneath her chin disappeared, showing clearly the ugly bruise on her neck.

Neck!

"Yup," the sheriff said strongly. "And she's dead."

The nagging in the back of my mind banged to the front. I knew suddenly what had been bothering me about necks, right from the moment I met Sarah on the bus.

"You may be wrong there, sir," I said calmly. "I think we can visit Delilah Abercombe right now."

CHAPTER 25

"Hello, Miss Abercombe," I called to the stooped figure peering beneath the building.

We had been ignored as we drove up.

"Please come out from there!" she pleaded instead to someone under the building. Distress was obvious in her voice.

Behind me, Sarah and Joel waited with the sheriff in his patrol car. Behind the car, the others—Mike, Ralphy, Uncle George, and Aunt Edith—waited in the pickup truck. They had agreed to let me speak first, alone, because all of us at once might be too much of a shock.

"What is wrong with you?" she cried again underneath the shack. "You've always been my friend."

I cleared my throat and tried again, slightly louder.

"Miss Abercombe?"

She did not respond. Could it be that I was wrong? That I had brought everyone out here on a wild goose chase?

I stepped closer.

"Miss Abercombe?"

Without turning, she said quietly, "I heard you both times. I only hoped you would go away. Something very distressful has happened."

"Miss Abercombe. We need you."

She turned to face me. "My friend has crawled underneath. He's never done that to me before. I'm afraid he's sick. And he's my only friend. Without him, my life is nothing."

"You can have other friends now, Miss Abercombe." I

pointed behind me. "All you need to do is tell the sheriff what Mr. Keyster did to you over fifty years ago. Then you'll never have to hide from anyone again."

She walked to within a foot of me and stared in my eyes. I tried not to flinch. I told her all that had happened in the cave.

"I believe you are telling the truth," she finally said. "I know you found the bank money. You must have found the rest of the pouch in the cave."

I nodded.

It had been a crazy two days. First, crying from frustration and rage when I believed Joel would die with me in the cave. Then, crying with relief after being rescued. Now, feeling the sadness of a person who had lived in fear of speaking to anyone for so long. I could see that once she had been very pretty. My eyes filled with tears.

"Yes, Miss Abercombe. The letter explained it all. If only you could have shown it to someone all those years ago."

"I looked, you know," she said. "But the creek bed changed completely during the storm. When I went back to get the letter, the cave was lost. Sealed over. Since then I've been here, looking for a way to get back in."

She almost collapsed. "And now my best friend is hiding from me, too."

I took her by the elbow.

Suddenly she looked very frail and vulnerable. "Will you help me get Samson? He's underneath the shack, you know. He's been there for over two days."

"Yes, Miss Abercombe. We'll make sure Samson is fine."

I hoped my eyes would be dry by the time she and I got back to the vehicles.

Epilogue

"Thanks for your help, Sarah," I said, admiring our hand-iwork. "It's amazing what you can learn from history books."

"Well," she said, "I've always wanted to see how the Indi-ans did it. Now I know. Those pegs are pretty effective, I would say."

"Very funny," Mike grunted as he pulled at the ropes. "You can let us go now."

"Sure, Mike. Sure."

He was on his back in the middle of the lawn in front of the ranch house. Uncle George and Aunt Edith were in town helping Miss Abercombe shop for women's clothing, so it had seemed like a good time to experiment.

The way the Indians did it was to put four pegs far apart into the ground, one for each of a person's arms and legs. The tough part for Sarah and me was sneaking up on Mike and getting the sack around his head so that we could carry him. It had also been a war to tie each arm and leg to a peg, but there he was, soaking up the sunshine and kicking help-lessly against the ropes.

"We'll let you go, too, Ralphy," Sarah promised. "Soon."

She sat back in her lawn chair to gaze at the two of them pegged securely into place. "More lemonade, Ricky?"

"Of course," I said from where I was reclining in my lawn chair. "One would hate to be without refreshments during the entertainment."

"Entertainment?" Ralphy moaned.

"Don't worry, you won't miss it," I replied.

"This morning," Sarah began as she relaxed in the sunshine, "what first clued you in to knowing that Quigley Spears was Delilah Abercombe?"

"Your neck."

"*My* neck?"

"This is going to sound strange, but necks kept coming at me. When I first saw you on the bus, your neck bothered me and I didn't know why. But that was when I thought you were a guy. Then Quigley's neck bothered me when I thought he was a guy. Once again, I didn't know why. When I saw the bruise on your neck this morning, I also remembered my necktie in church on Sunday. And all of it finally hit me."

"What, Ricky, what? You're driving me crazy with these stupid clues."

"In church it had occurred to me that a tie makes your Adam's apple feel like Adam's applesauce."

"Stupid joke," Mike called from the grass. "Adam's applesauce."

"I am ignoring all rude comments from the gallery," I said, then turned to Sarah. "So why would Adam's applesauce give me the answer?"

She laughed. "Because girls don't have Adam's apples."

"Bingo," I said. "The first time we met Quigley—I mean, Delilah Abercombe—she noticed me staring at her neck and quickly hid it with her handkerchief. She was very aware that she didn't have the required Adam's apple to pose as a man. When I put all of the 'neck' things together, that gave me the first big hint."

Another luxurious pause for a sip while Mike and Ralphy squirmed against the ropes.

"Then I started piecing things together. Remember in the gully I said that the phantom outlaw had to be Delilah herself? But then I disagreed with myself because we decided she couldn't live close by for over fifty years without someone seeing her. When it occurred to me that Quigley might be Delilah, suddenly the mysteries made some sense. Her shack was by the cliffs. It was the perfect place to explore the canyon until the day she found her lost cave entrance."

I paused. "And the most obvious thing was the name of her dog, Samson."

Mike gave me a puzzled look.

"Samson and Delilah," I explained. "The names go together. Like

Romeo and Juliet. Like Mike Andrews and Dummy."

"You didn't tie us here to lecture us on your brilliance," Ralphy said.

"Ah yes, Ralphy. You are nearby, aren't you? Tsk, tsk. What's going to happen when Joel comes by with his latest friend?"

Mike and Ralphy groaned.

"Your brother amazes me," Sarah said. "Crawling under the shack to get Samson and coming out with a family of little Samsons."

"There's irony for you," Ralphy said despite his discomfort. "Delilah, posing as a man for over fifty years, never dreamed Samson, too, was a she. *And* about to have puppies, as we should have guessed when we saw how big her belly was the first time we stopped by the shack."

Naturally, Joel had disappeared in the excitement of everybody meeting Delilah Abercombe. He had reappeared at our gathering near the truck, holding two puppies, and with Samson dutifully two steps behind him. Aunt Edith and Uncle George had decided right then to adopt one of the puppies.

"At least Delilah was relieved at that," I said, sipping on the lemonade. "Her longtime friend hadn't deserted her after all."

Sarah leaned back and stared at the far hills. "Just think. Over fifty years of prowling the Wolf Creek cliffs as a woman imitating a man imitating a woman bank robber." She giggled. "Did that make sense?"

"It would make sense to let us go," Mike commented without hope.

"In due time, young man," I told him gravely. "Mike, you, of course, remember certain farm cats and certain pillows filled with catnip? How someone named Ricky and someone named Sarah were afflicted every morning as a result?"

Ralphy and Mike moaned in unison.

I sighed in enjoyment of their moans, the sunshine, the lemonade, and the anticipation of what would happen when Joel next appeared.

During my sigh, I began to think about Miss Abercombe. As a young girl, Delilah Abercombe had once stumbled across the cave in the cliffs and had always remembered its location. After Keyster refused to return to her the phony letter of intent, she had robbed the bank, intending to prove her innocence and his fraud later. At first, after the robbery, it had been her intention to remain in the cave for several days until the posse gave up. Instead, she saw an opportunity to escape during the blinding storm. That was lucky for her, because when she returned several weeks later to get the papers, she could not find the entrance. It had caved in.

Proving Keyster's fraud then became her obsession. She waited long enough for the excitement to fade away, then returned as Quigley Spears and used the last of her money to buy land near the cliffs. That started her long search for a way into the cave, her long wait for the entrance to reopen.

Since as Quigley her hair was short, she purchased a blond wig to wear whenever she went into the cliffs. She didn't mind that people thought the area was haunted. It gave her more privacy as she roamed the cliffs. Waiting and hoping for a way back to her letter. Sometimes she wore shoes with horseshoes attached to leave tracks where no horse could possibly climb, which fooled people more.

She, of course, had never known we had seen her on that bright moonlit night. We never saw her tether her horse. We only heard her special shoes clanking down a secret path into the cliffs. Which of course sent us running. And when we met her, carrying the shotgun as Quigley, it was only because she was afraid she had actually hit us with the landslide, when instead she had just been trying to frighten us after hiding her horse and scooting up the cliffside.

"All's well that ends well. Keyster confessed, Delilah with her land back, us alive and glad for it," I said, breaking my own thoughts. "And look, here comes the reason this day will really end well."

Joel rounded the far corner of the house, proudly pulling Samson by the ear.

Aunt Edith and Uncle George had convinced Delilah Abercombe to move into the ranch house until she could find a nicer place to live than the shack. That meant Samson and her puppies had come along, too.

The sight of the huge black dog galvanized Mike and Ralphy into a frenzied bucking against the ropes.

"Our catnipping friends are nervous at the sight of a little puppy dog," I told Sarah cheerfully. "It's like they think we're looking for revenge."

Samson ambled behind Joel, panting happily. Her puppies were in the barn in a dry, warm bed. Motherhood and Joel had mellowed her completely. Mike's and Ralphy's eyes bulged as I continued. "Sarah, you do have the necessary ingredients for today's scheduled entertainment?"

"Certainly."

"Well, then. Now is a good time."

Sarah left her chair and applied gobs of chocolate icing to Mike's face, then Ralphy's.

"Joel," I said, "Mike and Ralphy really want to meet Samson."

Joel stepped over to them, still pulling Samson's ear, and smiled shyly.

"Funny place to sleep," Joel said.

Mike and Ralphy froze in arched fear, not daring to shake their heads free of the chocolate.

I took another sip of my lemonade.

"This is the life, isn't it?" I commented to Sarah as we watched the huge dog begin to slowly lick Mike's pinched face.

"It sure is, Ricky."

Then, right in front of Mike and Ralphy, she leaned over and kissed my cheek. "Especially with someone as cute as you. Thanks for helping me figure things out about my dad."

By the time I had recovered by untangling myself from my collapsed lawn chair, Samson had started on Ralphy's terror-stricken face. Sarah was still giggling. And Joel had returned with a pigeon to introduce to Samson.

I like summer vacations.